F.W.A

Veel 1

Signed

In the Lair of the Cozy Bear

Cyberwarfare with APT 29 Up Close and Personal
A Novel

Original title:
In het hol van de Cozy Bear

by F.W.A. van Nispen tot Pannerden

Translated from the Dutch
by T.H.E. Hill

T.H.E. Hill

WITH my compliments!

T.H.E.Hill

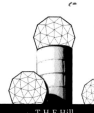

T.H.E.Hill

Signed

On the cover: the flag of the Netherlands; l337 Cozy 834Я (staff photo); coat of arms of the AIVD (via *Wikimedia Commons*, the use of this coat of arms does not imply an endorsement from the AIVD); Friend of the l337 Cozy 834Я (staff photo).

Library of Congress Cataloging-in-Publication Data
van Nispen tot Pannerden, F.W.A.
    In the Lair of the Cozy Bear: Cyberwarfare with APT 29 Up Close and Personal—A Novel
Original title: In het hol van de Cozy Bear / F[loris] W[illem] A[lexander] van Nispen tot Pannerden
Translated from the Dutch by T[homas] H[einrich] E[dward] Hill

ISBN-10: 1722475498
ISBN-13: 978-1722475499
First published in 2018

1−2−3−4−5−6−7−8−9−0

Contents

Guide to l337 S934k   v

The Ninth Floor   1

Happy Halloween!   9

Menno   17

Saskia   27

The Battle of Foggy Bottom   37

Let Them Eat Cake   47

The White House   55

Black Hat and DEF CON Briefing   65

A Big Contretemps   73

The RNC Hack   81

Cozy Bear Does The Pentagon   91

Bright Light City   99

Home Again   111

Cozy Bear Counter-hacked by CIA   121

A Delicate Problem   131

Floris and Saskia   141

Whack a Hack   153

Cross Bears   163

Summer in the Bear Lair   171
When You Come to a Fork in the Flowchart, Take It   181
Loose Lips Sink Ships   193
Epilogue   201
Afterword   203
About the Author   204

Bletchley Park:
"the geese that laid the golden eggs — but never cackled"
— Winston Churchill

Guide to
1337 S934k

1337 s934k (*leet speak*) is a cryptolect used by hackers to show that they are part of the 'in-crowd'. The term *leet* is a contraction of the word *elite* in the sense of *better than everyone else*. One of the key characteristics of 1337 s934k is the replacement of letters with numbers. The table below summarizes the most common replacements.

Numbers for Letters

0 (zero)	O (oh)
1	I
2	Z
3	E
4	A
5	S
6	G
7	T
8	B
9	P

No problem can be solved from the same level of
consciousness that created it.

— Albert Einstein

The Ninth Floor

I was in the Friday Division Team meeting, pretending not to be bored by all the team chiefs saying "Nothing to report." It had been a slow week.

It was just about my turn when the division secretary stuck her head in the door and pointed to me. This was against the Division Chief's very strict instructions. Nothing was ever to disturb him while he was holding a Division Team meeting. He glared at her with his best 'if looks could kill' scowl, but she didn't go away. That meant it must be something very important, like the building was on fire, or there was another revolution in Russia, or the Division Chief's wife was on the phone.

"What is it? Damn it!" growled the Division Chief.

"Mr. Holbrook is wanted on the ninth floor," said the secretary with all the awe that a summons to the ninth floor was due.

I had never known anyone who was summoned to the ninth floor, and I doubted that the Division Chief had either. In fact, I don't think I knew anyone who had ever been on the ninth floor.

"They said 'right now'," continued the secretary.

The Division Chief turned his scowl from the secretary to me. "What the hell have you been up to now?"

"Beats me," I replied. "Unless it was that little contretemps on Wednesday, but I didn't think that would get the ninth floor involved."

"What contretemps?" asked the Division Chief.

I started to answer, but the Division Chief said, "Tell me when — if — you get back. What are you still sitting around for?"

I made the most elegant hasty exit from the conference room that I could manage, by climbing up onto the table and walking across it to the side of the room where the door was. Charlie got up so I could climb down using his chair for a ladder. In my younger days, I'd have just jumped over Charlie, but discretion is the better part of valor, and Charlie knew it. We'd worked together off and on for more years than either of us cared to remember.

I headed for the elevator in the main tower that went all the way to the ninth floor where Daddy DIRNSA hangs his hat. On the way up in the elevator my whole working life flashed before my eyes. I considered all the things I'd done that had pissed people off. Well, some people need pissing off, because they are more concerned about office politics, political correctness, and empire building than about the collection of Intelligence that meets National Requirements. It was a fast elevator. It didn't stop anyplace else but the ninth floor. I was just getting to that little contretemps on Wednesday when the door opened.

The prim-and-proper secretary looked at the dirty sweater I'd had on for the last week, and then took in my matching wrinkled khaki pants. Her face gave the impression that she didn't think I belonged there, which I didn't, but, instead of pressing the button on her desk that called for security, she asked politely, "How can I assist you Mr. …?"

"Holbrook," I said. "You sent for me."

"Ah, yes," she said, as she got up from behind her desk, and walked over to a polished, real-wood door. She knocked once. This caused the door to produce a solid sonorous sound appropriate to these elevated spheres. Without waiting for an answer, she pushed the door open, said, "Mr. Holbrook, sir," and ushered me into a small, but plush conference room with two people in it. One of them was the Deputy Director. I'd seen his picture on the organizational chart you pass if you come in the 'Front' entrance. The other one I'd never seen before.

"Sit down, Mr. Holbrook," said the Deputy Director, motioning to the only other chair in the room. "This is Mr. Smith. You're here because we would like to talk to you about a Detached Service Officer (DSO) assignment to a third-party site."

That was a surprise. I was expecting to be drawn and quartered. I smiled politely, and took a seat in the leather-covered chair.

"Mr. Holbrook," said Mr. Smith, whose alias was about as obviously fictitious as they come, even in cheap spy novels. "Your record says that you speak both Dutch and Russian."

His accent gave him away. He sounded exactly like my father-in-law when he tried to speak English.

"Yes, we speak Dutch in the house," I replied in Dutch, eliciting a bemused smile from Mr. Smith, and a questioning

3

look from the Deputy Director. "My wife is from The Hague," I continued in Dutch.

"Yes, that's in your file," said Mr. Smith, "but it says nothing of how good your Dutch is."

We bantered in Dutch for about five minutes, while the Deputy Director ignored us with his nose in a file. When Mr. Smith discovered that we both liked the same pancake restaurant in Kijkduin, he felt that he had learned all he needed to know about my ability to speak Dutch.

"And your Russian?" asked Mr. Smith in English. "And, by the way, I don't speak Russian, so just tell me." The change of language brought the Deputy Director's nose out of his file.

"Better than my Dutch," I replied.

"That *is* good," said Mr. Smith.

"He'll do nicely," said Mr. Smith to the Deputy Director. "The other candidates were not at all suitable. They all spoke Dutch too poorly, and those expensive suits would be completely out of place where he will have to work."

The Deputy Director didn't look too pleased at this news, but he nodded in acknowledgement.

"Mr. Holbrook, this is an official offer of a DSO assignment to a closely held third-party project. Would you like to go? Yes or no."

"I might," I answered. "Depends on where it is."

"I can't tell you more about the project. It's very restricted knowledge. You'll only find out about it, if you accept the assignment."

"Yes, I understand all that. What I want to know is where I would be going to work this project."

The Deputy Director looked at Mr. Smith, passing the ball back to him.

"Zoetermeer," said Mr. Smith.

"*RampstadRail* Tram lines three and four out of The Hague?"

"I understand that that is possible," said Mr. Smith, "but I prefer to take my car."

"Of course," I said. "In principle, I'm agreeable. But I'll need to ask my wife. Can I tell you tomorrow?"

"We'd prefer to know today," said the Deputy Director. "We want you on site at the end of next month. Call your wife and ask her. You can use the phone in the outer office."

"For a closely held project, I think that would be poor operational security," I said, hoping to score points for security awareness without overplaying my hand. "Suppose I drive over and ask her face to face. It would take about two hours out and back, depending on the traffic."

Mr. Smith nodded his agreement.

"Come back *here* when you've spoken to her. I'll leave instructions for you with the secretary."

I didn't say anything about the short fuse on the reporting date to the Deputy Director. I figured this offer would not be repeated, even if I was the one that Mr. Smith liked. Kathy, on the other hand, said plenty.

"How can we possibly be there by the end of next month?" she asked.

"The plane ride is only eight hours," I said.

She didn't think it was funny.

"That gives us four weeks to get ready to fly. With a push from as high as the offer came from, I think all the bureaucratic gates will fly open for us."

I could see from the expression on her face that this wasn't going to win the argument for the assignment, so I cut to the chase. "This is a once-in-a-lifetime chance, and the price of admission is being ready to fly in four weeks. You want to live thirty minutes away from your parents or not?"

That was a rhetorical question. I already knew the answer, but it had to be asked, out loud and in person. That was part of the mechanism that made this partnership work. You had to have a chance to express your opinion before the decision was made. Approving a decision after the fact never felt as warm-and-fuzzy good as being asked beforehand.

Back at the Fort, I took the express elevator to the ninth floor, where the secretary greeted me with polite efficiency.

"Yes? Or No?" she asked.

"Yes," I said. "Kathy said to 'go for the gusto!'."

"Please read this, and sign where indicated."

T O P S E C R E T SAVOY
LIM/DIS NOFORN

The Computer Network Attack (CNA)-team of the Dutch Joint SIGINT Cyber Unit (JSCU), a collaboration between the Dutch Algemene Inlichtingen- en Veiligheidsdienst (AIVD, General Intelligence and Security Service) and the Dutch Militaire Inlichtingen- en Veiligheidsdienst (MIVD, Military Intelligence and Security Service) have gained real-time access to a computer network in Moscow at IP ███████████ being used by an Advanced Threat Actor (ATA, e.g. a nation-state).

This particular activity has been designated Advanced Persistent Threat (APT) 29, and has been assigned the covername Cozy Bear.

It is believed to be a Спец-группа Кибер-разведки и Атаки (Special Cyber Intelligence and Attack Group) of the Служба внешней разведки России (SVR, Russian Foreign Intelligence Service).

This source can only be discussed with those explicitly known to be cleared for access. In the event of doubt of someone's clearance status, the Access Control Officer who maintains the complete, current access list can be reached at tel. ██████ (secure).

Signature   Date

That explained why it had to be Dutch *and* Russian. I signed and handed the folder back to her.

"Here's a white shirt, a tie, and a sports coat," she said, pulling a pile of clothing from one of her desk's drawers, and dumping the stuff in my arms. "Go in the conference room and change."

She didn't sound like a lady to be trifled with, so I did as she ordered.

When I came out, I could see that she still had doubts about my wardrobe, but that didn't stop her from shoving a pass to the Executive Dining Room into my left hand. "The Deputy Director expects you at eleven thirty sharp. No classified conversation in the dining room. Don't slurp your soup, and keep your elbows off the table," she said, leaving no doubts about what she thought of me.

"I may have a few rough edges," I said, "but they don't keep me around for the way I look. I can make the equipment stand up and sing, and report what was in the song in six languages."

She didn't look entirely convinced, but she did soften her scowl a little.

Somewhere between the soup (cream of asparagus) and the main course (chicken tetrazzini), the Deputy Director said, "Having looked at your record, I have my doubts about you in this job. You seem to ruffle feathers everywhere you go."

"I only ruffle the feathers that need to be ruffled," I said. "Did you read past the complaints, which I'm sure are strategically placed at the front of my file, to the part where they talk about what I've accomplished? I don't have any doubts about me in this job."

"Neither did Mr. Smith," replied the Deputy Director. "He said you'd fit right in with his motley crew of cyber-pirates. I just wanted to warn you that my objection to your assignment will be a matter of record."

"Oh ye of little faith," I thought to myself.

"I get the picture," I said out loud. "If things go wrong, I'm on my own."

He winked.

"By the way. What happened to your dirty sweater?" he asked. "Mr. Smith told me that was one of the things that convinced him to ask for you."

"Your secretary. She wanted me to look presentable for the Executive Dining Room."

"Ah, yes. She would," he replied. "She's very efficient."

Happy Halloween!

The next stop after lunch was the secretary again. She was efficiency in spades. She already had my check-out sheet and a stack of PCS orders to hand me.

"Go get your time cards from your present division and bring them back to *me*," she said. "Passport photo and application appointment for both you and your wife is tomorrow at 10:00. Don't be late. You'll be travelling on 'official' passports. Your appointment at Transportation is at 11:00."

She went on like that for another five minutes, but I won't bore you with the details.

To make a long bureaucratic story short, we landed at Schiphol Airport at 07:35 on the morning of Halloween. It was a Friday, and I was counting on not going in to work until Monday, which would give us the weekend to get on local time. Every now and again things really do work out the way you planned.

There was a driver to meet us at the airport just outside baggage claim. The picture I'd been sent said his name was Kees. He started a 'welcome to Holland' spiel in serviceable English, but Kathy cut him short.

"It was a long flight, and I'm tired," said Kathy. "Please, just speak Dutch."

That seemed to take Kees by surprise, but he immediately switched into Dutch with a Hague working-class accent thick enough to cut with a knife. Kathy had an uncle who had been a cop in The Hague. He had the same accent. Now, if it had been Gronings or Limburgs dialect, I'd have asked him to switch back into English, but Kathy's uncle was a cool guy, and we'd visited them often enough that I could follow along fine.

Kees took us to our new home, which he explained was an accommodation address. "If any mail comes for Louise," said Kees, "just put it in a zip-lock bag and take it in to the office. Call the case officer on his secure line. It's the number in the bar code for the buy-one-get-one offer on the 'pizzeria' card by the phone. He'll come pick it up himself."

Kathy looked perplexed. She had never been exposed to operations before, but I smiled. I knew exactly what he was talking about.

Aside from that, it was a nice house in a respectable residential neighborhood.

Kees gave us a quick tour of the house. The house was completely furnished in government-issue modern, there was food in the fridge, both frozen and fresh; *and* the beds were made up. That's the kind of thing you really appreciate when you get off a trans-Atlantic flight, and the idea of a nap is very appealing.

"Within walking distance of the office," said Kees, "there's a route drawn on this map."

There was a note in English, paperclipped to the map that said:

> *Rest up over the weekend. You both have to come in on Monday, but don't come in before 09:30, otherwise you'll get caught up in the morning rush. Tell the guard at the gate to call Marieke in HR, and she'll come out and get you. Marieke is efficient, but it will take most of the morning. She will have you sign for the house, get you your ID cards, your visas, and stuff like that. You can have lunch in the building cafeteria, or in Stadshart Zoetermeer across the road, where there are several good places to eat.*
>
> *The afternoon will be all work, so your wife won't need to come back to the office. Just show your badge to the guard at reception and ask him to call me at ████ (secure).*
>
> *Cheers, Floris.*

"Anything else you need before I go?" asked Kees.

Kathy and I were too tired to think of anything to ask. It might have been a whirlwind tour, but Kees was very efficient.

"You having a car shipped over?" asked Kees.

"No, we thought we'd just get a second-hand car, something that would be reliable transportation," I replied.

"In that case," said Kees, "my brother Hans runs a car dealership. Just call him at this number," continued Kees, handing me a business card, "and he'll come around, pick you up and show you what he's got available. Tell him I sent you, and he'll give you an extra special good deal."

"Kees and Hans *Kortekaas*?" said Kathy, looking over my shoulder at the business card. "I thought I recognized you, but just couldn't figure out from where. You used to live on Stevinstraat in Scheveningen, right?"

"Yes."

"And you had two sisters: Annemieke and Marloes."

"Yes."

"I'm Katja van der Kerk. We lived just down the street."

"That's why you speak Dutch," said Kees. "I'd never have recognized you. How long's it been?"

"We won't go into that," said Kathy.

"We'll have to get together and talk over old times," said Kees.

"I've got Marloes's eMail address. I'll arrange it with her," said Kathy.

"Tell her 'no more than 40 people'," said Kees with a wink. "She thinks that anything less than a hundred isn't worth the effort."

"Oh," said Kees, when he turned the handle of the front door to let himself out, "there's candy here for the 'trick-or-treaters' who'll be coming tonight," pointing to a bowl on a small table near the door. It was a big bowl.

"Trick-or-treaters?" asked Kathy. Trick-or-treat wasn't a thing in Holland when she was growing up, nor when our daughter was growing up for that matter.

"Yeah," said Kees. "This is a family neighborhood with a lot of kids. They'll come around and knock on the door, and say 'Trick or Treat,' you know, just like in America."

"Yes, we know how it works in America. We just didn't know that it had caught on over here," said Kathy.

12

"It sure has," said Kees. "Some people think it is just another excuse for the stores to sell stuff, and others are afraid that it will turn the kids into pagans or wiccans, but I think it's fun for the kids. What I want to know is why didn't we do Halloween when I was a kid?"

We thanked Kees, and gave him a piece of Halloween candy. He smiled in thanks, and waved as he drove off.

It was a big bowl of candy, but there were only four pieces left on the bottom after the last trick-or-treaters rang the bell at just short of nine p.m. There had been an almost constant flow of kids big and small; with and without parents from the time it had started to get dark. There had been a selection of super heroes, princesses, pirates, ghosts, witches, bumblebees, and fairies. It had been more fun than in our neighborhood in the States.

By the time Monday rolled around, we were on Dutch time (more or less), had seen Kathy's parents three times, and all her siblings at least once (there are seven of them). We had bought a car from Hans (he gave us a really good deal), and gotten Dutch SIMs for our cell phones (Kathy's niece knew 'the best place' to go).

We had a late breakfast, and strolled into the office. Even at our relaxed pace, it was less than ten minutes away. Marieke was as efficient as Floris had said. Read this and this and this. Sign here, and here, and here.

"Here's your permanent badge and both your laminated IDs," said Marieke in Dutch. "Your visas, driver's licenses, and insurance cards have to go out to be processed by the actual offices that do them, but I should have them back on Wednesday, Thursday at the latest. I'll give you a call to come pick them up," she said.

"Don't tell me," I replied. "I have to sign for them."

"You catch on quick," said Marieke. "Nice to have met you. Our cafeteria is not as bad as some people pretend. It's on the ground floor. Just look for the signs when you get out of the elevator. Today's special is *nasi goreng*[1]," she said, after running her finger down a menu on the bulletin board near the door to the hall.

"Let's have lunch here in the cafeteria," said Kathy. "It's probably the last chance I'll get to look around inside the building."

It wasn't the best *nasi goreng* I've had, but it wasn't the worst by a long shot. It was a lot tastier than you might imagine for a place that feeds ███ people every day.

I walked Kathy home. She took the car to go visit her sister and some school girlfriends that afternoon. We agreed to meet at home for a quiet evening, and probably call it an early night, because being on Dutch time is a relative thing for the first week you're in town after coming over from the States.

I hiked back to the office, showed my new badge, and had the guard at the gate call Floris. He came out to the lobby to collect me about five minutes later. He was tall, like many of the Dutch of his generation. He had brown hair, blue eyes and an athletic build. He was wearing faded, pre-stressed jeans, and a black T-shirt that said:

There are only 10 kinds of people in the world, those who understand binary, and those who don't.[2]

---

[1] Translator's note: *Nasi goreng* literally means "fried rice" in Indonesian. It is a common dish in Holland, a reminder of the time that Indonesia was a Dutch colony, much like why curry dishes are popular in England.

[2] Translator's note: For those who do not understand binary, in binary, the glyphs '10' represent the quantity *two*.

Hacker T-shirts look the same whether the hacker is working on the Linux kernel, pulling down the big bucks maintaining an old COBOL bank program, or breaking into a TOP SECRET server somewhere. A hacker's black T-shirt communicates the wearer's status to other hackers. While a hacker may claim that an old, threadbare T-shirt signals his or her disdain of what passes for high fashion in mainstream society, what it in fact signals is a status that is conferred by conforming with high hacker fashion.

Floris didn't look all that pleased to meet me. It was, after all, his project, and I was — as far as he was concerned — an interloper. He motioned me to follow him, and we headed back to the project spaces, stopping just in front of a door to a shielded enclosure.

"Cell phones have to go in one of these lockers," said Floris in English, pointing to a bank of lockers on the wall next to the door. "Absolutely no cell phones are allowed in the office!"

His English was quite good, and even though I was sure he'd been told I speak Dutch, I played polite by responding in the language he'd started this conversation in: English.

"If you leave your phone on, and place it in the locker with the screen up, when you get an alert on your phone and the screen lights up, the alert will be passed to the annunciator in the office with the number of the locker you put your phone into. It's a simple light sensor arrangement with a one-way filter on it."

I put my phone in locker number 9. It had my name on it, done by one of those label machines.

Floris showed me the cypher lock combination.

"No writing that down," he said, as if I would. I'd memorized and forgotten a few thousand more of these than he had, and had done the same spiel myself a few thousand times as well, but I wasn't going to tell him that. I just shook my head in acknowledgement.

It would take a couple of days before I could work the combo without looking. By that time, it would be more muscle memory than a conscious recall of the numbers I needed to push.

I swung the release lever on the door with an ease that comes with years of practice.

"Heads-up, everybody," said Floris in Dutch. "This is Mark Holbrook. He's the American they've saddled us with. You can all introduce yourselves to him as you get a chance."

Maybe he did not know how well I could speak Dutch. That was a pretty impolite thing to say to somebody's face.

Menno

"Menno has 'The Watch'," said Floris, switching back to British-accented English. "Menno, put your hand up so he can see where you are."

A hand went up off to the left, and I headed over that way. While my first thought was that I was being palmed off on an office flunky, I was really being thrown into the deep end of the project. Menno was a waterfall of Dutch, Russian, and English words full of facts and code.

The person attached to the raised arm got up to get me a chair as I walked around to where he was. He was about my height with green eyes and carefully coiffured dark hair.

He had on the 'uniform of the day' black T-shirt, but his was freshly laundered and ironed. It said:

I code, therefore I am

With an eCartesian philosophy like that, I had the feeling that we were going to get along.

His name had other philosophical associations for me as well. The only Menno I knew of before I met him was Menno ter Braak, the man considered the 'conscience of Dutch literature' who had been an enormous influence on Dutch intellectual life in the period between the two World

Wars. Ter Braak was the man who advanced the individualist ideal of the *honnête homme* (Man of Integrity) who refuses to conform to other people's expectations and systems.

"Cool T-shirt," said Menno in Moscow-accented Russian as I turned to stick out my arm to shake hands with him, allowing him to read my T-shirt. "I'm a fan of Clarke's." My T-shirt said:

Any sufficiently advanced technology is indistinguishable from magic

I was impressed. It's not everybody who recognized this T-shirt as a quote from the 'Third Law' formulated by the British science fiction writer Arthur C. Clarke. Later that afternoon, I heard Menno explaining it to Floris.

"We call this 'The Watch'," said Menno, switching to American-accented English, "because we can actually see into the entrance to the Bears' Lair. This monitor," he continued, pointing to a screen on the right of his chair, "is the video feed from a camera focused on the hallway that leads to their vault door. The insert at the lower left corner is the video of the close-up camera used to ID people who ring the doorbell to request access, or who work the combo on the door."

"I saw the mugshot books from the ID camera back at the Fort," I replied. "A veritable 'Who's Who' of SVR[3] VIPs, some of whom have never been photographed before, with identifications confirmed by their badges. Pretty neat."

---

[3] Translator's note: The SVR is the successor organization to the KGB. SVR stands for Служба внешней разведки России (Russian Foreign Intelligence Service).

"Here comes Sasha now," said Menno, pointing to a figure walking down the curved hallway towards the camera. "He's the project leader. He took a late lunch."

"I've never seen the hallway image," I replied, keeping my eyes on the figure moving in the camera's direction.

"That's the other cool thing," said Menno. "I know where that hallway is. It's in the basement of the university building in Moscow, off Red Square, where I was for a study-abroad semester two years back."

"I've never seen that in any of the reports," I said.

"They won't take my word for it," said Menno. "And I didn't take any pictures of it while I was there, so it won't be reported until we can figure out a way to confirm my ID of the hallway."

Sasha finally got close enough for me to read the text on his T-shirt—black, of course. It said:

If brute force doesn't solve your problems, then get a bigger hammer

The need for a bigger hammer to make brute force attacks work on crypto systems had driven computer developments from the 'bombe' that Turing designed to crack the Enigma key settings, and the Colossus computer designed to attack the Lorenz radio-teleprinter code to the ... Hmm, that's one of those 'If I told you, I'd have to shoot us both' stories, so we'd better leave it at that.

Sasha worked the combo on the door and let himself in. The hallway was empty again.

Menno made an entry in the log-book for the door.

"There's a video motion detector watching these feeds that logs any movement in the hall whether this position is manned or not," said Menno. "It flags the time in a log, and records the video as long as it detects any motion so we can see who or what it is that caused the event."

"What do you mean 'what' caused the event?" I asked.

"Well, there's the cat and the mice it chases," replied Menno. "They're active from about zero-two hundred to zero six hundred Moscow time. 'The Ghosts', as Saskia calls them, are active around the midnight hour. The system logs a motion event, but you can look until your eyes cross and not see anything."

"Did you think about a sag in the local power grid making the lights dim, or the ultrasonic motion detectors in the hallway fluctuate? Either of those could trigger a video motion event."

"I'll mention that to Saskia," said Menno. "She's the one who normally deals with 'The Ghosts', I mean overnight motion events."

"Were there extra 'Ghosts' on Halloween?" I asked, tongue in cheek.

"Let's see," said Menno, seemingly missing the joke implied by my question.

His fingers flashed over his keyboard, and an event log filled the screen in front of him.

"There were twenty motion events Halloween night between 21:00 and 03:00 Moscow, while the three-day running average before that was two. I hope they put out candy for the ethereal trick-or-treaters."

Trust a hacker to take a joke as far as it will go and then some.

"The screen below the hallway is the feed from the Bears' own video motion detector," continued Menno. "It gives us a view of their shielded enclosure from a point just opposite the main door. They turn off the camera when they come in, but a 'bug' that Saskia wrote into the software turns it back on without the motion detection logger. You can't read any of their screens or documents, but it does let you see what is happening in the enclosure."

"Who's the girl whose rear end Sasha has his hand on?" I asked.

"Very observant," said Menno. "That's Natasha."

"Are they a number?"

"Sasha thinks so, but she doesn't. If he doesn't remove his hand, in about thirty seconds, she's going to hit him."

She did.

"This screen over here," said Menno, pointing at the one to the left of his chair, " is what we call 'Bear Chat'. This is their internal chat channel that connects all the positions. It gives us a written overview of what's going on in the lair."

As if on cue, a message in Russian popped up on the screen from the user with the avatar 'circle B'.

"Boris, are you going to get that obfuscator routine to me before the anniversary[4] of the Great October Revolution?"

---

[4] Translator's note: The Great October Revolution took place on 25 October 1917, according to the Julian calendar (old style), but after the calendar change instituted by Lenin in 1918, it was celebrated on 7 November according to the Gregorian calendar (new style). The same disconnect is seen in the Russian dates for Christmas, which falls on 25 December according to the Gregorian calendar (new style), but is celebrated by the Russian Orthodox Church on 7 January, which is where Christmas would be on the Julian calendar (old style).

"I'm working on it, Sasha," replied the user whose avatar was 'circle Б'. "It's just about there."

"Let me put that in context for you," said Menno.

"Please do," I replied.

"Boris has been working on a routine in Assembly Language for over a week, and he can't find the bug that makes it crash intermittently. Saskia found it the first time she reviewed his code. He doesn't have a filter to prevent a divide by zero in front of a polynomial calculation."

"I can see how that could be a problem," I replied. "Why can't one of the other Bears review his code?"

"Sergej is the only other person on the project who can do Assembly Language, and he's been on leave for the last week."

"That sort of makes sense," I said. "But why is Sasha on Boris' case? Can't he wait until Sergej gets back from leave and can take a look at the code?"

"That has to do with Sasha's avatar," said Menno. "The letter 'Б' in his avatar stands for Вождь (Vozhd', Leader)."

"As in the nickname for Stalin?" I asked.

"Yes, that's about right," said Menno. "He has delusions of grandeur."

"I've had bosses like that. No fun at all. How's Floris?"

"He's reasonable enough, but he does try to live up to his posh 'van … tot' surname once in a while. Nothing to really worry about. If he sticks his nose too high up in the air, we just sic Saskia on him, and that mellows him out," replied Menno.

"Getting back to the Bears," I prompted, after Menno had been silent for about a minute.

"We also have audio from the intercom microphone for the main door," said Menno. "Comes in handy. Not all the Bears like to 'chat' via the keyboard. It goes on to a digital recorder that you can access from any terminal in this room."

"You have digital clean-up filters for the audio?"

"A full set, and you need it when they're across the room from the mike, but you can usually understand everything well enough."

"Got something you can call up for me to listen to?"

"Sure. Just put on the headphones."

"Sasha, get your (expletive) hand off my ass, or I'll slug you," said a female voice.

"That was the last thing in the queue," said Menno.

"The Cozy Bears run a sophisticated operation," continued Menno. "Their preferred method of intrusion is a carefully researched, targeted spear-phishing attack that carries, or links to a malicious dropper," said Menno, as if he were reading from a script, but I couldn't see anything on-screen or on his desk that he could be reading from.

"The dropper, or the payload, immediately runs a threat analysis to ensure that it is not being analyzed on a virtual machine with a debugger, is not located on an Admin user's machine, or in a sandbox. It then runs checks for a variety of security software. If any of these threats are present, the dropper or payload exits, leaving no tracks, because it only runs in volatile memory and doesn't make any writes outside the memory area it reserves."

"That's pretty cute," I said. "How does the payload get the permissions it needs to run?"

"It runs under the permissions of the user whose account has been pwned[5]."

"What kinds of lure documents do they use?"

"Weaponized Word.doc files, image.png files, PDF-s, and ZIP files."

"And what does the payload do if it deploys?"

"It opens an encrypted command and control channel over HTTPS so that the Bears can remotely control the victim computer. Once the payload has a foothold, it is very persistent. The Bears like to camp out on a network undetected for long periods of time, expanding their access to data they can exfiltrate."

"What do they do to achieve persistence?"

"They have a variety of persistence techniques to avoid detection and prolong the usable life of the implant that they apply at random intervals to change the implant's profile. For example, their implant variants are signed with bogus Intel and AMD certificates, and they can change which one is displayed remotely."

"One of the shortcomings of their technique that we've noticed is that they run some of their routines live during Moscow office hours, out of normal office hours for the victim computer. One of the first things we check when we run counter measures is if the logs show unusual activity, especially out of office hours."

---

[5] Translator's note: *pwned* is hacker jargon for *owned*, indicating that the hacker has taken control of a device. This usage originated with a typo in the on-line game *Warcraft*. When the program beat a player in a battle for a piece of territory, it was supposed to display this piece of territory "has been owned." Instead it said: "has been pwned." The letters 'O' & 'P' are right next to each other on the QWERTY keyboard.

"If that's a giveaway, how do you keep your implant's low profile during the time difference of office hours between us and the Bears?" I asked. "We're ZULU plus 1, and Moscow is ZULU plus 3."

"Our implant only runs out of hours using named and hijacked scheduled tasks that will look perfectly normal on the logs," replied Menno. "For the most part, since we have six hours of overlap, we tend to do most of our collection live. If we suspect something important will be going on, we can have someone come in two hours early to give us real-time coverage from the start of the Bears' day in Moscow."

"What's with the covername?" I asked, figuring that if anybody would know, it would be Menno, what with all the other trivia at his fingertips. If he knew, he'd be the first person I'd run into who did.

"I get the 'bear' part," I said. "Bears have been used to symbolize Russia in political cartoons since around the sixteenth century. The mascot for the Moscow Olympics in 1980 was a cartoon bear named Миша (Misha). But where did 'Cozy' come from?"

"That's because the trinomial 'COZ' shows up a lot in the Base64[6] strings that they use for their implant," said Menno. "Saskia noticed that when she was running regressions of the strings, before she figured out it was Base64."

"Of course," I said, wondering how long it would have taken me to figure out that it was Base64.

---

[6] Translator's note: *Base64* refers to a binary-to-text encoding scheme to represent binary data as an ASCII string. Commonly, the 64 ASCII characters used would be ASCII A–Z, a–z, and 0–9 for the first 62 values. The remaining two characters vary between implementations. Base64 was originally a work-around for transmitting data via information systems that were not 8-bit clean, like eMail once was.

Saskia

"All your talk of 'Saskia this', and 'Saskia that' makes me want to meet her. Can you introduce me? Your girlfriend?"

"No," replied Menno. "My girlfriend's named Sylvia. She's a lot more girlish than Saskia."

"My wife's name is Kathy," I replied with what I hoped was an air of comradery. "I'll let you know how girlish she is compared to Saskia once I've met Saskia."

We got up and walked over to a desk in the far corner of the shielded enclosure. The person (I hesitate to say woman) sitting behind the desk was small (petite didn't seem to be the right word), but full of energy. The back of her T-shirt—black, what else?—said:

Binary Four

That's definitely not a feminine T-shirt slogan. *Binary Four* is hacker jargon for 'The finger,' as in *digitus impudicus*. The origin of this expression is allegedly taken from a visualization of the way to write *four* in binary (00100) and its similarity to the position of the fingers of the hand when displaying 'The Finger.'

"Sas," said Menno in Dutch, "our American said he wanted to meet you."

"Menno told me so much about you that I wanted to see the person behind the stories," I said in Dutch.

She turned around to glare at Menno.

The front of her T-shirt said:

CAPS LOCK
Preventing Login Since 1980

The two 'C'-s in the top line of her T-shirt were strategically placed to highlight her femininity.

"He's only been saying good things about you," I said quickly before she could make the glare more vocal or tangible, which seemed to me a very probable outcome at the moment. "Like how you spotted the bug in Boris' code."

She looked at me in silence for a minute.

"My dad said he picked you up at the airport," responded Saskia without the same heavy Hague working class accent as her father. "He said that he and my aunts and uncle knew your wife when they were kids in Scheveningen," she continued, shifting her expression from glare to inquisitiveness.

"Yes. That's right," I replied. "Small world isn't it?"

"So what are you here for?" she asked, cutting to the chase. "To enjoy a retirement tour close to your wife's family, or to do some work?"

When he heard that question, Menno, who had been inching away from Saskia so as to escape back to 'The Watch' stopped. The answer to Saskia's question was obviously one that he'd like to hear himself.

"Yes, and yes," I replied. "A marriage is a partnership that requires you to think about what's good for your other half. This will be a good tour for Kathy: payback for some of the less pleasant places we've been. She deserves it."

"And the work?" prompted Saskia impatiently.

"I'm looking forward to it. I expect it to be fun."

"Are you just here to spy on us, or is there something you can do for the mission?"

"With the ten-minute introduction to the mission I've had from Menno, I'm not exactly sure what I can do, but I've got a long track record of thinking of imaginative ways to improve collection. But while I'm thinking of something to help your collection effort, I'm also here to edit the English in your reports so that no one will be able to tell they were written by someone whose first language is Dutch. That will keep people who read the reports from guessing that they came from this room, and perhaps blabbing about it. *And* I'm the person who will be endorsing your requests for funding, training, and equipment."

By this time Floris, along with most of the other members of the team, had his ears glued to my conversation with Saskia.

"We need an ST-1," interjected Floris, trying unsuccessfully to suppress a leer.

I know a newk trick[7] when I hear one, especially one this old, but I played along.

"I'll submit a request for an ST-1 for you," I said. "Anything to keep the project going full steam ahead."

---

[7] Translator's note: a *newk trick* is a trick played on naïve people new to the operation.

It was hard to keep a straight face while I said it, but I think it worked, because about fifteen minutes later I could see Floris whispering in Saskia's ear, and she doubled up with laughter. It took about thirty minutes for the 'joke' to work its way around the whole team. They were sure I was stitched up, and were now waiting for the flamer to come back from the Fort in response to my request for an ST-1.

That night on my way home, I stopped by a little shop that did plastic name plates while you wait, and ordered one that said: "ST-1 — Precision hacker headspace calibration device."

After dinner, Kathy and I drove over to a garden supply shop, where I picked up a fairly large, decorative stone. It weighed about a kilo. I figured that was enough to adjust even a stubborn hacker's headspace.

Kathy still hadn't gotten the joke yet, and I had to spell it out for her. "The designation ST-1," I said, "is a language joke that works in either Dutch or English. When written with all letters and no numerals, ST-1 becomes S-T-E-E-N or S-T-O-N-E."

Kathy didn't laugh, but she smiled real wide. At least she doesn't groan at my jokes like our daughter.

When we got home, I glued the plastic name plate to the stone, and put it in a nice box we'd found in the hall closet. The next morning, I took it in to the office with me.

Floris was in what he called "percolation mode," with his eyes closed, and his feet up on the desk, typing one-handed on the wireless keyboard in his lap, holding a cup of coffee in his left hand. His T-shirt said:

Hackers are devices
for converting caffeine into code

"Floris," I announced in an over-loud voice that even the team members with earbuds in could hear, "they overnighted your ST-1 out as soon as they got the request. Nothing's too good for our Dutch hackers with the most-est."

He sat upright, dropping his feet to the floor, spilling his coffee in the process, thankfully, not on his keyboard. It only got his T-shirt, which was black with white lettering, so it wouldn't show too much; and his artistically stained pants, which he said were only just beginning to feel lived in. It being Tuesday, he wasn't due to put on a clean pair until Saturday.

I plopped the box down with a solid thud on his desk.

"Go ahead and open it," I said, looking around the room to make sure I had an audience for this little comedy skit. I did.

Floris sat there for a moment, trying to decide what to do.

"Go ahead and open it, Florisje[8]," said Saskia. "You asked for it."

Floris stood up, and opened the box. He looked inside and promptly sat down again. Saskia came over and reached inside to take the ST-1 out so everybody could see it. "Come look what it says on the name plate," she called.

Floris was a red as a beet.

"Hey, man," I said, "I'm not just some suit who came over from the States to keep an eye on you. I've been around

---

[8] Translator's note: *Florisje* is the diminutive form of the name *Floris*.

31

the block a few times, and know a thing or two. I was telling newks to go get me an ST-1 before you were a twinkle in your father's eye. ... Your coffee cup's empty," I added, picking it up off the floor where it had fallen. "Let me get you a fresh one."

I left the team to admire the ST-1, and waited until they had all gone back to their own computers before bringing Floris his coffee.

"That's heaviosity," he said.

"A lighter one wouldn't do the job as well," I replied.

"OK, Mr. 'been around the block a few times,' wrap your head around this!" said Floris, hurling down the hacker equivalent of a gauntlet. "I've got a 200-character block of data in the packets from the Moscow server that are all white-space, just non-printable characters. What's it doing in there?"

"Can I see it in Unicode?" I asked.

Floris' fingers flew across his keyboard, and the screen changed to a list of Unicode characters.

```
[U+200B][U+200B][U+0020][U+200B][U+200B]
[U+2003][U+200B][U+0020][U+0020][U+2003]
[U+200B][U+2003][U+2003][U+0020][U+2003]
[U+2003][U+2003][U+0020][U+200B][U+200B]
[U+2003][U+0020][U+0020][U+2003][U+200B]
[U+2003][U+200B][U+0020][U+200B][U+2003]
[U+0020][U+2003][U+200B][U+0020][U+0020]
[U+200B][U+2003][U+200B][U+0020][U+200B]
[U+0020][U+200B][U+2003][U+0020][U+2003]
[U+200B][U+200B][U+0020][U+0020][U+2003]
[U+0020][U+200B][U+200B][U+200B][U+200B]
[U+0020][U+200B][U+200B][U+0020][U+200B]
```

```
[U+200B][U+200B][U+0020][U+0020][U+2003]
[U+200B][U+2003][U+2003][U+0020][U+2003]
[U+2003][U+2003][U+0020][U+200B][U+200B]
[U+2003][U+0020][U+0020][U+200B][U+2003]
[U+0020][U+200B][U+2003][U+200B][U+0020]
[U+200B][U+0020][U+0020][U+200B][U+200B]
[U+200B][U+0020][U+2003][U+2003][U+0020]
[U+200B][U+2003][U+0020][U+200B][U+2003]
[U+200B][U+0020][U+2003][U+0020][U+200B]
[U+0020][U+200B][U+2003][U+200B][U+0020]
[U+0020][U+2003][U+0020][U+200B][U+200B]
[U+200B][U+200B][U+0020][U+200B][U+2003]
[U+0020][U+2003][U+200B][U+0020][U+0020]
[U+2003][U+0020][U+200B][U+200B][U+200B]
[U+200B][U+0020][U+200B][U+0020][U+0020]
[U+200B][U+2003][U+0020][U+200B][U+200B]
[U+200B][U+2003][U+0020][U+200B][U+0020]
[U+200B][U+2003][U+200B][U+0020][U+200B]
[U+2003][U+0020][U+2003][U+2003][U+200B]
[U+0020][U+200B][U+0020][U+0020][U+2003]
[U+200B][U+200B][U+200B][U+0020][U+200B]
[U+0020][U+200B][U+2003][U+0020][U+200B]
[U+2003][U+200B][U+0020][U+200B][U+2003]
[U+200B][U+2003][U+200B][U+2003][U+0020]
[U+0020][U+200B][U+2003][U+0020][U+200B]
[U+2003][U+200B][U+200B][U+0020][U+200B]
[U+0020][U+2003][U+200B][U+200B][U+2003]
[U+0020][U+0020][U+0020][U+0020][U+0020]
```

I looked at the screen for a couple of minutes, before the light went on in the enormous dark cavern of my mind. "Piece of cake," I said. "Chocolate even. It's old world comms in new world coding. It's manual morse in Unicode, using a zero-width space for a 'dot,' an em-space for a 'dash,' and a regular space for a space, with two regular spaces between words, and five regular spaces at the end to pad to an even 200 characters."

"Morse?" said Floris.

"Yeah, manual morse code," I replied. "Named for Samuel F. B. Morse who invented the telegraph."

Floris had the Wikipedia page for Morse Code open before you could bat an eye. He opened a 'Find and Replace' dialogue box, and swapped all the [U+200B]s for periods and all the [U+2003]s for hyphens.

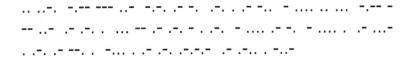

Ignoring me completely, Floris started transcribing the dots and dashes into Latin letters, using the morse code chart he had open in a separate window on his screen. The morse message said:

"If you can read this, you are smarter than the average bear. Alex."

"Hey, Menno," said Floris, "weren't you talking about how morse code is a technodinosaur that had outlived its usefulness in the twenty-first century? Come take a look at this!"

"Yeah," said Menno, as he sauntered over to where Floris was. "Dead and gone. Nobody uses it anymore."

"That's what you think," said Floris, pointing to his screen. "You know all those 200-character blocks of white space we've got? They're morse code. Look!"

Menno stood there with his mouth hanging open while Floris explained how it worked.

"Who'd a thunk?" said Menno. "A signature block in morse code. Real retrotudinal squared."

I had taken Floris down a notch with the ST-1, but having been around the block more than a couple of times also teaches you how to build your team back up again after a fall. I casually headed back to my terminal to give the crowd behind Floris' back a chance to see the screen properly, so he could climb up a couple of rungs on the ladder of esteem.

"Hey, I can write a routine to automate the conversion, and we can feed them all in," said Menno, who ran back over to his terminal, where he began flailing at his keyboard to write the routine before someone else beat him to it. This was, after all, a room full of hackers.

An hour later, he was regaling us with the 'Easter Egg'[9] signature blocks he had 'decrypted.'

To boldly go where no man has gone before. Natasha.

When you come to a fork in the flow chart, take it. Igor.

You've been pwned. Enter any 11-digit prime number to continue. Boris.

I shud report you to the code police for incompetence. Sasha.

The team at Cozy Bear had a sense of humor. Well, we all thought so.

---

[9] Translator's note: An *Easter Egg* is computer jargon for a secret feature or message hidden in a computer program on the analogy of looking for Easter Eggs left by the Easter Bunny.

The Battle of Foggy Bottom

It looked like just another Friday afternoon with things winding down towards quitting time, but it turned into a 'Friday the thirteenth' even though the calendar said it was the fourteenth. Kathy and I were planning to go to Gouda on Saturday for the annual *Sinterklaasintocht* (Santa Comes to Town Parade), when Sinterklaas (Dutch Santa) officially arrives together with the hordes of Black Peters who accompanied him on his 'trip from Spain' (the Dutch Santa has the good sense not to live at the North Pole where it's cold) to visit the good boys and girls of The Netherlands.

Like the Macy's Thanksgiving Day Parade, the *Sinterklaasintocht* marks the beginning of the festive season with wish lists in (wooden) shoes put out for Black Peters to put presents in — Santa supervises things from outside on his horse, for whom carrots are provided. We hadn't been to one of these in years, and were looking forward to it. Last time we had been was when our daughter was still young enough to enjoy it.

Our daughter was a big fan, because, being half Dutch and half American, she always got presents from both Sinterklaas on December fifth, and Santa on December twenty-fifth.

Sjoerd was complaining about having to make another pot of coffee, but those were the rules: the person to take the last cup had to make the next pot.

"Is anybody gonna want another cup of coffee?" asked Sjoerd. "It would be a waste to make another whole pot with only an hour to get before we call it a day."

"I don't know about that," said Saskia, who was on 'The Watch' position that kept track of things at Cozy Bear in real time. "The bears don't look like they're going home, and it's an hour past their normal quitting time. Sasha just posted a message on Bear Chat, asking who wants pizza and who wants burgers."

"Sounds like a prelude to an all-nighter," said Floris. "Looks like we're gonna get some overtime. Better start that next pot, Sjoerd. And check that there's enough coffee in the supply cabinet."

"You know that this is the weekend of the G20 in Brisbane. Maybe they're hoping to get in on that," said Menno, always a source of insightful trivia.

"Igor says that he only wants pizza if they are going to Сбарро (Sbarro)," said Saskia.

"There's one on the other side of Моховая улица (Mokhovaya Street) opposite the МГУ (Moscow State University)," said Menno, our resident expert on the geography of Moscow who'd done a semester there to polish up his Russian.

"Natasha says if they're going to Бургер Кинг (Burger King), then she wants луковые колечки (onion rings) instead of картофель фри (French fries)," continued Saskia.

"The closest Burger King is the one at the World Clock Fountain, just a block north of the Sbarro," chimed in Menno. "It was popular with the students."

"That's eight pizzas, and ten burgers," reported Saskia. "If we're going to keep them company, maybe we should order out, too? I could go for some *nasi goreng*."

When the 'negotiations' over what to order settled, the team's take-away order was for eight *nasi goreng* (Indonesian rice), extra *pindasaus* (peanut sauce), twenty-four *saté* skewers, half and half chicken and pork, four big *loempia*s (Indonesian egg rolls), and don't forget the *kroepoek* (Indonesian shrimp crackers). Simon, however, wanted a dozen Vietnamese *loempia*s from the stand in front of the Hema, which was OK, because it wasn't out of the way to Bij de Toko, where the others wanted to order from.

Indonesian food is real popular in Holland. It's a leftover from the time when Indonesia was a Dutch colony. I don't think you can find a Dutch town so small that it doesn't have an Indonesian restaurant. It's very tasty.

One by one folks left the shielded enclosure briefly to call their significant others.

"Hi, Kathy," I said. "I'm gonna be late, because I have to save the world again."

"Any idea how late?"

"The team just ordered Indonesian take-away, so it could be real late."

"And I thought that this was going to be a nice quiet assignment where the world didn't need to be saved quite so often. Any chance that there will be explosions and gunfire?"

"If there are, it won't be near here."

"Yes, I know that this is the stuff that promotions are made of," said Kathy. "And I'm proud of you for being so good at it, but it's mighty damn inconvenient sometimes."

"Yeah, I know, and I love you too, Honey. Just remember that it pays the rent on that house in Holland that we thought we'd never get. I'll call if I get a chance."

"Sasha just walked in with a stack of pizza boxes," said Saskia, keeping us posted on the latest from 'The Watch.' "I'm getting hungry. What's keeping Sjoerd and Simon?"

"Anything happening on the server?" asked Floris.

"Aside from somebody dropping a slice of pizza on a keyboard; nothing," said Saskia. "By the way, the image of the boxes of pizza that Sasha was carrying shows an address. It's the one you thought it was, Menno."

"And there was much rejoicing," said Menno, a true Monty Python fan, if I ever saw one. "The time that it took him to walk there, and back, plus the address of the pizza place is another confirmation of my location of the Bear Lair."

"Igor just got back from Burger King," said Saskia. "Where are Sjoerd and Simon?" she asked as Simon shouldered his way through the door into the shielded enclosure with a plastic bag full of food in each hand.

"We decided that we needed beer to go with the nasi goreng," said Sjoerd. "You can't have nasi without a beer. *Eet smakelijk*! (*bon appétit*!)"

"I'll do the report of the timing of the walks to the take-aways once I finish my loempia," said Menno.

"Any chance they could have driven?" asked Floris.

"None. There's no place to park where they are, unless you're a lot bigger wheel than peons like them who man the place."

"Be sure to put that in the report," said Floris, "for the mundanes, of which, unfortunately, there will be many who read it."

"There should be an anti-idiotarianism law to keep people like that out of positions of responsibility," said Menno through a mouthful of loempia.

"The Bears just released that batch of spear-phishing eMails they've been crafting," said Saskia, "the ones addressed to people at the US State Department."

"How many had we counted?" I asked while pulling up an OPS IMMEDIATE report form on my terminal.

"153," said Floris.

IMMEDIATE
T O P S E C R E T SAVOY
LIM/DIS NOFORN
SUBJ: Incoming Cozy Bear Phishing Attack
14NO14 16:01Z
Cozy Bear released a volley of 153 spear-phishing
eMails addressed to recipients at the US Department of
State.

The malware payload is a known infected Flash video
called "Office Monkeys LOL Video.zip," which will in fact
play a humorous video of chimpanzees wearing ties in
an office setting. While the video is playing, the package
drops and launches a malicious executable named
"CozyDuke.exe," which enables a backdoor through
which Cozy Bear can exfiltrate data to their server.

CozyDuke components escape normal anti-virus detection, because they are signed with bogus Intel and AMD certificates.

I clicked 'Send,' and got a success message: "Your report has been sent."

"I wonder if that will get anybody's attention in D.C. at lunch time on a Friday," I silently asked the infinite void, which, as expected did not answer me, but Floris did.

"I doubt that anybody in Washington will notice," said Floris. "It's Friday and they're all out to lunch."

"Hope springs eternal," I replied.

"A drizzle of in-coming encrypted data packets for the Bears just popped out of The Onion Router (TOR) from somewhere with an IP of ███████," said Saskia.

"Let's see where it is," said Menno, lazily typing what I guessed was a DNS[10] query.

"BINGO, Mark," yelled Menno joyfully across the enclosure to me a minute later. "It's the static IP for the US Department of State in Washington, D.C.."

That was my queue to click open another OPS IMMEDIATE report blank and start typing.

IMMEDIATE
T O P S E C R E T SAVOY
LIM/DIS NOFORN
SUBJ: Indication of the Success of the Cozy Bear

---

[10] Translator's note: The abbreviation DNS stands for Domain Name Server. This is, in essence, a 'telephone book' for the internet, as it hosts a database of public IP addresses and their associated hostnames.

Phishing Attack
14NO14 16:08Z
Cozy Bear has begun receiving encrypted data packets
from a static IP address correlated with the US State
Department.

"Data packets coming out of TOR have stopped," said Saskia from 'The Watch. "Sasha is pissed off. I think his last post to Bear Chat was 75% profanities. I've never seen most of those words before."

I got up and walked over to 'The Watch' to read Sasha's post to Bear Chat. "Yep, those are profanities. I haven't heard anybody talk like that since I was listening to a bunch of drunken Russian sailors. He ought to wash his keyboard off with soap."

"Hey, Floris, I told you somebody in D.C. would pay attention," I said as I passed his position on the way back to my computer.

"It only took them two hours and how many follow-up reports?" parried Floris.

"Sixteen," I said, as I started typing follow-up #17.

IMMEDIATE
T O P S E C R E T SAVOY
LIM/DIS NOFORN
SUBJ: Cozy Bear Phishing Attack Follow-up #17
14NO14 18:03Z
Cozy Bear expressed markedly profanity-laden
displeasure that reception of encrypted data packets
from the IP of the US State Department has terminated.

IMMEDIATE
T O P S E C R E T SAVOY
LIM/DIS NOFORN

SUBJ: Cozy Bear Phishing Attack Follow-up #19
14NO14 18:13Z
At 18:06Z Cozy Bear instructed the open-source 'Meek'
Domain Fronting obfuscation plugin for TOR to reroute
to a new reflection server. Reception of encrypted data
packets from the IP of the US State Department
resumed after 6 minutes at 18:12Z.

"Hey, can you provide us some cover back there?" I typed in an informal to my contact at the Fort. "We don't want the Bears to think that someone is looking over their shoulder as they attack the system at State. Can you have someone, or multiple someones at State send some eMails complaining about how the IT people are messing around with the system and giving them grief?"

About a half hour later, Sjoerd, who had relieved Saskia on 'The Watch', said: "Boris just sent a round-robin on Bear Chat about three eMails he'd seen from people at State complaining about IT running maintenance on the system during the day. He thinks that's what happened to the feed from State."

"Thanks for the smoke screen," I typed to my contact at the Fort.

"Keep those follow-ups coming," was the reply. "We're hanging on your every word back here."

IMMEDIATE
T O P S E C R E T SAVOY
LIM/DIS NOFORN
SUBJ: Cozy Bear Phishing Attack Follow-up #26
14NO14 19:16Z
Cozy Bear has begun to receive encrypted data packets
from the IP of The White House.

Analyst Comment: Since we have seen no phishing eMails directed at The White House during this attack, can only assume that someone at State forwarded the malicious eMail to an acquaintance at The White House.

IMMEDIATE
T O P S E C R E T SAVOY
LIM/DIS NOFORN
SUBJ: Cozy Bear Phishing Attack Follow-up #36
14NO14 19:34Z
Cozy Bear told the implant sending encrypted data packets from the IP of The White House to go to sleep and await further instructions.

IMMEDIATE
T O P S E C R E T SAVOY
LIM/DIS NOFORN
SUBJ: Cozy Bear Phishing Attack Follow-up #49
14NO14 22:18Z
At 22:12Z Cozy Bear instructed its Domain Fronting obfuscation plugin for TOR to reroute to a new reflection server at IP ███████████. Reception of encrypted data packets from the IP of the US State Department resumed after 5 minutes at 22:17Z.

IMMEDIATE
T O P S E C R E T SAVOY
LIM/DIS NOFORN
SUBJ: Cozy Bear Phishing Attack Follow-up #78
15NO14 16:23Z
Cozy Bear stated in no uncertain, profanity-laden terms that the victim computer had shut down. Cozy Bear expressed the hope that the victim computer would reboot from the 24:00 Local Washington time back-up, as that would preserve the Bear's penetration.

IMMEDIATE
T O P S E C R E T SAVOY
LIM/DIS NOFORN
SUBJ: Cozy Bear Phishing Attack Follow-up #81
15NO14 17:46Z
Cozy Bear stated the victim computer should have rebooted by now. Since no new encrypted data packets were being received from the victim computer, Cozy Bear declared the attack failed. A heavy object was thrown across the room, barely missing a member of the Cozy Bear team, who was more than a little upset. He advised the thrower (the team leader) to "Hack 127.0.0.1."

Analyst comment: This is a hacker euphemism instructing the person to whom it is directed to perform an impossible, unnatural act upon himself. The IP address 127.0.0.1 normally designates the computer's own network services, sometimes called the localhost.

IMMEDIATE
T O P S E C R E T SAVOY
LIM/DIS NOFORN
SUBJ: Cozy Bear Phishing Attack Follow-up #82 and Final
15NO14 18:45Z
The Cozy Bear team has secured their operations area and gone home.
Tired but unbowed, the reporting officer and his team are preparing to do the same.
Palmam qui meruit ferat.

"We used up all the coffee," said Sjoerd. "I bought the last five pounds. Whose turn is it to buy more?"

Let Them Eat Cake

I stopped in at Bakkerij Jongerius on my way into the office on Monday, and ordered a cake with an orange keyboard decoration over the text "*Je maintiendrai*" (I will maintain …[11]), the motto of the Dutch Royal family. I thought it was a good way of saying 'Thanks' to the team for their extra effort throughout the night on Friday and the day on Saturday. If you don't tell people they did something special, they'll think you take them for granted. The Battle of Foggy Bottom was something special.

The cake would be ready at lunch time. Just before picking up the cake from the baker, I stopped by the florist, where I picked up a stack of *bloemenbonnen* (Flower Gift Cards); two for everyone. This is Holland where they say "Flowers like People. Take some Home today." I got Flower Gift Cards, because 1) I couldn't carry eighteen bouquets of

---

[11] Translator's note: With reference to a letter of 1565, from Prince William of Orange, in which he explained the meaning of the motto as:

I will maintain virtue and nobility.

I will maintain the prestige of my name.

I will maintain the honor, the faith and the law

Of God and the King, of my friends and of myself.

tulips and a cake at the same time; and 2) because I knew that there weren't enough vases in the office to put them all in. The team could pick their flowers up on the way home, and they'd still be fresh when they got there.

I put the cake on the table near the coffee pot.

"That's a cool cake," said Menno. "What's it for?"

"To celebrate our victory at the Battle of Foggy Bottom," I said with as much pomp and flourish as I could muster.

"Where's 'Foggy Bottom'?" asked Saskia.

"Sorry," I replied. "'Foggy Bottom' is the insider's nickname for the US Department of State. It may not look like it today, but Washington D.C. was built on a swamp, and the place where they built the headquarters building for The State Department was known as 'Foggy Bottom'."

"And flowers for the victors," I said as I passed out the 'good for a bunch of tulips' cards.

"Great," said Menno. "I needed something to give to Sylvia to apologize for having to work last weekend. This will work just fine."

"Same here," said Saskia. "I'm having dinner with my parents tonight, and I can give them to my mom."

"I'm having dinner with myself tonight, and I can give them to me," said Sjoerd, always the life of the party.

Saskia glared at him.

"I'd like to do something more for the team," I said to Floris, between mouthfuls of cake, "but I don't know what would be most appreciated."

"Hackers," said Floris, "like everybody else, like a little extra money. Any chance of a cash award?"

"Not a lot," I replied. "I can't recall a single time that a DSO got a cash award from the Fort for someone at his Host's."

"Hackers are also motivated by a chance to play with new toys. We've been trying to get some slots in those hacking courses that you run at the Fort," said Floris, "but we haven't been having any luck. I've put in applications, but they've never gotten anywhere."

"I'll see what I can do," I replied, turning the idea over in my mind. The tumbling idea tried to regain its balance, grabbing at an old memory as it fell, landing on its feet.

"How does funding for a TDY[12] to 'Black Hat' and 'DEF CON' in Las Vegas for next summer strike your fancy?"

"Now that would be a treat," said Floris. "You think you can swing it?"

"It's a lot more realistic than me trying to get the Fort to pay for the cake and flowers I brought in."

I whipped off an informal to my contact back at the Fort with the subject line of "Applause for the Troops?".

My contact wrote back almost immediately. "People here were really thrilled with the way you stayed with the target all the way through the Battle of Foggy Bottom. Some people in high places are even saying you won it. I think if I put your request forward today, nine course slots and funding for three TDYs to Black Hat and DEF CON are practically a done deal."

---

[12] Translator's note: The abbreviation TDY is government jargon that means *Temporary Duty*. A *TDY-er* is a traveler who is on Temporary Duty, on loan to the receiving unit.

I had a formal message with nine firm course slots and a funding cite for the three Vegas TDYs by Wednesday.

"You'll have to foot the bill for the travel and per diem to the Fort for the courses out of your own budget, Floris, but the three TDYs to Vegas are fully funded, travel and registration and course fees," I said.

"Yeah, I think I can swing the money for the nine course trips," said Floris. "The hard part will be deciding who gets to go to Vegas."

We put our heads together for the rest of the afternoon, trying to figure out an equitable way of divvying up the laurels, but we couldn't think of a way that wouldn't disappoint the people who didn't get to go.

I was complaining to Kathy over dinner about how hard it was to decide who goes and who doesn't, and just like she always does, she found a solution.

"You put all the names in a hat, and hold a drawing. You don't decide, the fates do, and you hold out the promise of another trip to Vegas in next year's budget."

"Just another one of the few thousands reasons I love you," I said.

"Whatcha think, Floris," I asked the next morning after I explained Kathy's idea.

"We could write a program to generate a random number string and the TDYs go to the first three to recover the polynomial that generates the string," said Floris.

Trust a hacker to look for a way to lower the river rather than raising the bridge.

"Floris," I said, "first of all, if I wrote it, even with my 1337 skills, it wouldn't stump these guys for more than three minutes, while if you wrote it, you couldn't go to Vegas, and you at least deserve a shot. Secondly, Murphy's Law applies to your idea just like it applies to any other computer program. If there's any way that the program can go wrong, it will go wrong and in such a way as to cause the maximum of confusion to the maximum number of people all at once. Taken to its logical conclusion, that means that they would all solve the hash at the same time and would be pissed off that we didn't have funding for everyone."

"You have a better idea?"

"Yes, we do what Kathy said. Write all the names on identical pieces of paper, and draw three of them out of a burn bag."

"Who does the drawing?"

"I do. It's my treat, and I'm not eligible to go."

The winners were Saskia, Menno, and Simon.

That evening on the way home I brought Kathy a bouquet of tulips with a card that said:

> They also serve who only sit and wait.
>
> Thanks for waiting while I save the world now and again, and for pitching in to help clean up after the fighting's over.

The next morning when I came in, Floris flagged me down before I could even go get a cup of coffee.

"You see the news?" he asked.

"What news?" I asked innocently. "I haven't seen anything that looks work-related, if that's what you mean."

"There's a Russian website streaming live video from thousands of what people thought were private web-connected cameras with views of living rooms, bedrooms, driveways and even a stable, without the owners knowing," said Floris. "The site lists 1,576 cameras here in Holland, 4,591 in the States, 584 in the UK, and 870 in Japan. They are showing things like the view of a playground with a pool and trampoline here, a woman working out on a treadmill in a gym in Manchester, a couple making love in Arizona."

"No, I haven't," I replied. "Where's it at?"

"All the wire services have it, the papers here, the British tabloids," said Floris. "My concern is that it will alert the Bears to our video access."

"Is it in *The Washington Post*?" I asked. "I'll bet the Bears read *The Post* religiously."

"It's too early for *The Post* to be out," said Floris.

"Then we've got time to gather a little more information before we panic," I said. "Let's go ask Sjoerd. He's got all the technical ins and outs at his fingertips."

"I don't think so," said Sjoerd. "The cameras the Bears are using are *not* one of the brands that the article says were compromised, and the Bears did reset the password for their cameras from the factory default, which is the key to defeating this hack."

"Maybe it will make them nervous, and they will reset the password again."

"They can reset it all they want," said Sjoerd. "We don't need the password. We're seeing the video coming off their host, not direct from the cameras. Besides, their cameras are hardwired to the host, and this hack only works on wi-fi enabled cameras, so I don't think they'll be worried."

It took until the following Monday for *The Post* article to make it to the Bear Lair.

"Hey, Igor! You see this article in *The Post*?"

"Which article?"

"'How a Russian Website Peers into Your Home, and Your Baby's Room, by Hacking Webcams'. It's in the 'Morning Mix' section."

"That doesn't count as a hack," said Igor. "They're only accessing cameras that have passwords still set to the manufacture's default. It's like not locking the doors to your car when you park it on the street. Nobody's fault but your own if it's gone when you get back."

"To be good, a hack doesn't have to put a camel through the eye of a needle, it just needs to work," countered Sasha. "You see a way to piggy-back off this 'so-called' hack to do something we could use?"

"A Distributed Denial of Service attack is the first thing that springs to mind. It would be easy to get the cameras to ping the target," replied Igor. "I'd have to go through the manuals to do something more elegant, like pushing a phish through the eye of a camera."

"Why don't you do that," said Sasha.

"You see?" I said, when I showed Floris the transcript of the Bears' conversation. "You got worried for nothing. They didn't even think of their own cameras."

The White House

The Bears were down in the dumps about the failure of their penetration of The State Department computer system. They had been bouncing ideas around trying to guess what went wrong for over a week. The idea that it had been a result of IT support running maintenance on the system had its supporters and detractors, but nobody suggested that their operation had been penetrated, which made all of us feel much relieved.

The Bears launched a feverish round of reviewing all their code, tweaking their obfuscation routines, and setting up new reflection routers. Saskia and Sjoerd were tickled pink (well, maybe pink wasn't the right color for either of them: Sjoerd was too macho, and Saskia wasn't girlish enough). They had each found a vulnerability in the Bears' new code that we could exploit. Floris and I were hard at work on the justifications for a cash award for each of them from the AIVD. We had decided that if the recommendations were written in English and signed by both of us that they'd have a better chance of being approved. Being in American English would make it stand out from the rest.

Thanksgiving was coming up, but neither Kathy nor I felt like roasting a turkey and trying to find people to help us eat it. Leftover Thanksgiving turkey sandwiches are great, but not when you're still eating them after the first week in December. Besides, roasting turkeys are not that easy to find in supermarkets in Holland, and I didn't feel like driving to the American Military Commissary in Schinnen just to get one.

"Why don't you work Thanksgiving," suggested Kathy, "and take a comp day on the fifth of December when Sinterklaas comes and we'll go to my sister's."

That sounded like a good idea, because I knew better than to say 'no', and because her sister's grandkids would be there, and helping kids enjoy Sinterklaas is always fun.

When I showed up on Thursday, Sjoerd was already on 'The Watch', reading through the posts accumulated on Bear Chat between their open and ours, which was two hours later. He was doing curls with a five-kilo barbell in his left hand as he read, but he wasn't a dumb jock. He could quote Spinoza, Nietzsche, *Star Trek*, and Monty Python.

His T-shirt appealed to my linguistic sense of humor. The front said:

This T-shirt is
buzzword-compliant

The punch line was on the back:

Buzz Bomb (V1)
Buzzer
Buzz saw
Buzzard
Buzz Lightyear

As I walked behind him on my way to the coffee pot, I noticed that his coffee cup was empty. It is a truism of hacker culture that hackers run on caffeine. I offered to get Sjoerd another cup of coffee. I was sure that he had already had at least one.

"Sure, thanks," he said.

When I got back with his coffee, he was curling the barbell with his right hand. "You're going to love this," he said, as he took the cup of coffee in his left hand. "The Bears are going to wake up the implant at The White House today. Boris says that there won't be anybody above the rank of flunky on duty in the IT shop, and whoever has the duty will be more interested in watching the American football matches on TV than in keeping an eye on the system, which will probably be deserted in any event."

"Everybody watches the parade in New York, then eats too much, then watches football on TV," said Boris in his post.

I had to admit that Boris knew American culture pretty well.

"I hope I can prove Boris wrong," I said to Sjoerd. "After I report what the Bears are up to at The White House, somebody should get called in to take care of it. I've lost more than my share of Thanksgivings to operational call-ins."

"I've been in the States for Thanksgiving," said Sjoerd. "My money's on Boris' interpretation of the situation."

"Money?" said Menno, who had wandered over to see what was interesting enough for Sjoerd and I to be having a conference this early in the morning. "Let's start a pool for the persistence of the penetration."

Menno ran the office soccer pool, which was more of a social institution than a betting syndicate. The stakes were low, and if nobody had the correct pick, the money in the pot went to the coffee fund, which always seemed to be in the hole financially.

Nobody would take any date in the pool earlier than Monday. I took both halves of Thursday and Friday for €4 to show my patriotism, and next Wednesday afternoon and Thursday morning because it was only €1 more, and nobody had change for my five-euro bill.

IMMEDIATE
T O P S E C R E T SAVOY
LIM/DIS NOFORN
SUBJ: Impending Activation of Cozy Bear White House Implant
27NO14 07:28Z
Cozy Bear has stated the intent to activate the implant at The White House that was the result of an overflow from their attack on the US Department of State on 14 November.
The implant was successfully exfiltrating data on 14 November before Cozy Bear put it to sleep so that they could concentrate on the penetration of The State Department.
See my:
Cozy Bear Phishing Attack Follow-up #26 (14NO14 19:16Z)
Cozy Bear Phishing Attack Follow-up #31 (14NO14 19:26Z), and
Cozy Bear Phishing Attack Follow-up #36 (14NO14 19:34Z).

IMMEDIATE
T O P S E C R E T SAVOY
LIM/DIS NOFORN
SUBJ: Cozy Bear White House Implant Follow-up #12

27NO14 10:38Z
The Cozy Bear implant at The White House is exfiltrating OFFICIAL USE ONLY information on the current and future travel plans of PotUS[13].

When we closed up shop at the end of the day on Thursday, the implant was still active. When we opened up on Friday, there was a "Black Friday" surprise for us courtesy of the Bears.

IMMEDIATE
T O P S E C R E T SAVOY
LIM/DIS NOFORN
SUBJ: Cozy Bear White House Implant Follow-up #28
28NO14 09:58Z
The Cozy Bears remarked with great glee that they had intercepted an order for an HD, large-format, flat-screen TV at an incredibly low 'Black Friday' price from The White House computer. Their intercept had included the unencrypted credit card and CVV (Card Verification Value) numbers for (a named US person) placing the order. The Bears debated whether to order something for themselves with the credit card, but decided against it, because "the order would never go through with a 'ship to' address in Russia."

IMMEDIATE
T O P S E C R E T SAVOY
LIM/DIS NOFORN
SUBJ: Cozy Bear White House Implant Follow-up #36
28NO14 11:58Z
The Cozy Bear implant at The White House is exfiltrating eMails to and from PotUS. None of the

---

[13] Translator's note: The abbreviation PotUS is government shorthand for *President of the United States.*

eMails seen thus far contain CLASSIFICATION markings. Addressees include US diplomatic facilities and named US diplomats.

I wanted to come in over the weekend to keep reporting on the Cozy Bears in The White House in real time, but that was shot down by Floris, and confirmed in writing by the Director when I protested. He sent down a memo that said:

> Since there has been no indication of a readiness on the part of the Americans to act in real time on our Cozy Bear reporting of the penetration of a computer at The White House in Washington, D.C., I cannot in good conscience authorize overtime to continue reporting in real time over the weekend. Nor will I authorize DSO to work in project spaces alone over the weekend.

Like the song says, "you gotta know when to fold 'em," and this seemed like one of those times. I'd given it my best shot. I hadn't gotten what I asked for, but a memo on paper (even if it was in Dutch), along with a stack of situation reports, would go a long way to protect me from the inevitable fallout that would follow the bureaucratic explosion when the day weenies got back from the Thanksgiving Day weekend and found out what was going on at The White House, and what had not been going on back at the Fort.

I at least got Floris to agree that Sjoerd and I could come in two hours early at Cozy Bear open on Monday and start processing the collection from the weekend. Sjoerd came in with a thermos of coffee and a sack full of cheese and egg sandwiches. The Dutch normally don't do cheese and egg sandwiches, but Sjoerd had picked up the taste when he was in the States. Sjoerd went right over to 'The Watch,' started reading Bear Chat, and curling his five-kilo barbell left-handed.

I had orange juice and bacon-egg-and-cheese sandwiches that Kathy had made the night before. The bacon might have been American from the Commissary, but the cheese was Dutch. The Dutch do cheese right. Enough old Gouda cheese, and anything tastes good.

"Just because you're crazy enough to volunteer to go in to work at six in the morning, doesn't mean I have to get up at five to fix you breakfast, even though you're going in to save the world," said Kathy as she put my sandwiches in the fridge the night before.

I got comfortable at my terminal, and started digging through the accumulated materials from over the weekend. The last "Follow-up" in the reporting series on Friday had been number 58. I picked right up where I'd left off.

IMMEDIATE
T O P S E C R E T SAVOY
LIM/DIS NOFORN
SUBJ: Cozy Bear White House Implant Follow-up #59
01DE14 05:32Z
On Saturday (29NO14), the Cozy Bear implant at The White House exfiltrated memos written for PotUS on policy and legislative issues. The highest CLASSIFICATION marking of any of the memos seen thus far is CONFIDENTIAL.

"Nothing on Bear Chat to indicate that they're having any kind of problem with the implant," said Sjoerd. "And I can see more data packets coming in from it."

That wasn't particularly reassuring. My glass-half-full perspective had said that the implant would be toast by now. On the other hand, my glass-half-empty perspective had said that Boris, Sjoerd, Floris, and the Director were all right, and Washington was awash in a Thanksgiving/Black-Friday liberal leave policy, which meant that things would continue as is until the tide of people on leave turned.

I got on the opscom to my contact back at the Fort.

"He's on leave until Wednesday," said the fingers of the unknown person at the other end. "He flew out to California for Thanksgiving."

"Anybody back there cleared for COZY BEAR?" I asked.

"What's that?" asked the fingers.

"If I told you, I'd have to shoot you," I said. "I'll call him back on Wednesday."

It was slow going, a lot of stuff had built up over the weekend. I was still digging out on Tuesday, and the implant was happy as a clam in mud at high tide.

IMMEDIATE
T O P S E C R E T SAVOY
LIM/DIS NOFORN
SUBJ: Cozy Bear White House Implant Follow-up #99
02DE14 15:43Z
The Cozy Bear implant at The White House attempted to access the control settings for the secure Blackberry used by PotUS. Access failed at the log-in screen for lack of the required password.

By going-home time on Tuesday, I was up to "Follow-up #113".

My contact at the Fort normally got in at 08:00 Washington time; that's 14:00 Local Dutch time. I gave him ten minutes to hang up his coat and log in to his terminal. He answered right away.

"Hi, it's me, your friendly COZY BEAR DSO," I typed. "You seen my reporting on the implant at The White House?"

"What reporting?"

"The reporting with 137 'Follow-ups'," I replied. "The White House implant has been exfiltrating data since Thursday, and it's still running as we speak, dumping even more stuff to report in my lap."

"I'll get back to you," he typed, and the line went dead.

He didn't get back to me before Dutch close of business, by which time I had made it to 'Follow-up #153'.

The next morning, Saskia called me over to 'The Watch.'

"You're the one with the big vocabulary of Russian profanities," said Saskia. "Tell me what Sasha is so mad about. I can't figure it out."

"Well," I said, having studied his longish post, "he's more than a little displeased that they lost contact with the implant at 24:19 Moscow time. ... that's 16:19 Washington time."

"You won the pool," said Saskia.

I took Kathy out to dinner.

Black Hat and DEF CON Briefing

Floris booked a conference room for the briefing, because we'd be handing out cell phones, and we could not do that in the enclosure.

"You're going to dive into the deep end of Wild West Hackerdom, and it's going to be wilder than you can imagine. You have to be the best version of you every minute of every day for the whole week. It's not easy. It'll be 'Shields up, Mr. Spock', and 'More power to the shields, Scotty' the whole time you're there. I've been there, done that, and got these badges to prove it."

I had on one each of my old Black Hat and DEF CON badges, and shook them for effect.

"Lesson one." I said. "Don't do what I'm doing today," I said, launching my spiel. "Don't wear your Black Hat and DEF CON badges at the same time. Your Black Hat badge will have your name on it, while the DEF CON badge is anonymous. If you wear both, you'll make yourself the target of every practical and malicious jokester in the place."

"Do not tell anyone that you are from the AIVD," I continued, "because, even though there are lots of Intel people there, their laptops and phones are generally more aggressively targeted, because everyone wants to pwn your stuff to see what the 'spooks' are up to. Besides that, there are certain cliques, especially at DEF CON, who will be downright nasty to Intel people."

"Are we going to be 'under cover'?" asked Saskia with a gleam in her eye. "You know, like *Mission Impossible*?"

"Sorry to disappoint you," I said. "Your 'cover', thin as it is, is that you are from SecurITy, BV,[14] a Dutch IT Security firm. If anyone should call the number on these business cards I'm handing out, they'll run into an operator who can only speak Dutch."

"Supposed the person calling speaks Dutch?" asked Menno.

"If the person on the other end happens to speak Dutch, then the operator will say that you're out of the office on a job at the client's location. In any event, the system will harvest the Caller ID, and the call will be traced. You're the only people who have this number, so any incoming calls will be a reaction to one of these business cards."

"I only got nine cards," said Simon.

"Sorry," said Floris. "They aren't all for you. That's three for each of you. Just take the ones with your name on them."

"Three?" said Menno.

"The cards are not for you to paper over Black Hat and DEF CON," said Floris, "but to get you out of uncomfortable conversations where someone is pestering you for a

---

[14] Translator's note: The Dutch abbreviation BV (*Besloten Vennootschap*) is a legal construct similar to the American LLC, the English Ltd. or the German GmbH.

business card and won't take 'no' for an answer. If you run into someone like that, be sure to get their business card and report the incident in your trip report."

"What happens if I get into more than three situations like that?" asked Menno.

"If you're that unlucky, which we don't expect you to be," I said, "you say that you only brought 50 cards, and hadn't expected to need that many. Sorry, they're all gone."

"The place will be full of spooks, so it's normal for people not to say much about where they work, in fact, it's sort of a faux pas to ask people where they work. Nor is it unusual for people at DEF CON to decline to give their last names for security reasons."

"Next: Do not call the office for any reason, because it would break what little 'cover' you have," I said. "This next card has my number and Floris' number on it. If there's a work-related emergency, call."

"I don't see any telephone numbers," said Menno. "This is just a customer rewards card for a grocery store."

"Yes," said Floris. "The 'customer number' at the bottom under the bar code is fourteen digits long. The first seven digits are my phone number. The second seven digits are Mark's number. These are both cell phones, so, from the States, just dial 1316 plus the seven digit number. 1 is the international access code in the States. 31 is the country code for Holland, and 6 is the trunk code for cell phone numbers here."

"What do you mean by 'work emergency'?" asked Simon.

"A 'work emergency' would be a CIA or SVR case officer trying to recruit you," Floris replied.

"You're making it sound like *Mission Impossible* again," said Saskia.

"No," I interjected. "We don't really expect that you will need to call one of us about work, but prior planning prevents poor performance."

"If there's a life threatening emergency," I continued, "the American emergency number is different than the one here in Holland. Dial 911 for the police, ambulance, or fire."

"Speaking Dutch provides a limited level of privacy, but not 'encryption'. Don't fall into the trap of thinking that nobody around you speaks Dutch. For example, one night Kathy and I were in the States in line to buy tickets for a movie, and we were making uncomplimentary comments in Dutch about a couple in front of us in line, and the couple behind us said they agreed with us. The Dutch blend in very well in America. There will undoubtedly be some besides you at Black Hat/DEF CON."

"It may sound counter intuitive," I said. "You're going to one of the premier tech conferences in the world, but leave your laptop at home. Take some pens and notebooks instead. Not only can someone hack your laptop, or 'shoulder surf' while you use it, it can be stolen."

"And don't take you normal cell phone! It will be hacked, and all the personal data you have on it compromised. That's why we're giving you each a burner phone with pre-paid minutes on it.

These are for emergencies and letting the folks you leave behind here know that you are safe and sound. Do not activate them until you arrive in Las Vegas. The SIM cards are for an American carrier, and won't work over here."

"I want the red one," said Menno.

"Most vendors only take cash instead of credit cards, because the place will be awash with people who know how to make fake credit cards," I said.

"I read that during Black Hat, but especially during DEF CON, the ATMs in Las Vegas might be hacked or fitted with a skimmer," said Menno.

"Yes, we thought of that," I replied.

"You can get American dollars from the cashier here before you go," said Floris. "Your travel orders have been notated with 'Per Diem advance in local currency authorized.' You just have to tell the cashier a couple of days before that you want dollars so they will be sure to have that many on hand."

"You will, however, need to have a credit card with you when you check in to the hotel to confirm that you are the person who made the reservation, and for emergencies. We are, therefore, giving each of you an RFID-Blocking credit card holder for all your chip-enabled cards. On a normal trip, you probably wouldn't need one, but you're going to a place where there will be people anxious to try out their new sniffers on the attendees. I've seen multiple presentations on the schedule for this summer to demonstrate how easy it is to read credit card data remotely. You won't be the only ones with these holders."

"Menno, you want the red one, right?" asked Saskia.

Menno nodded 'yes'.

"If you are determined to ignore my sage advice and take a laptop, and/or fancier phone than the burner we gave you—we want those back, by the way—you may find yourself on "The Wall of Sheep," I said as ominously as I could.

"'The Wall of Sheep' is a big display that they put up at DEF CON where the names of users whose devices have been hacked, along with the type of device and the name of the app, are displayed, followed by the user's truncated password to show that they are not joking about having hacked your device or connection.

"Don't connect to any public wi-fi network. It's a reasonable assumption that every network you can see on your device is either intentionally hostile or has been compromised. The safest thing to do is avoid the Internet for the week. Don't check your eMail, your bank account, or anything you need a log-in for.

"You'll be swimming in a sea of people who all think they know more than you do, and some of them might be right, others might be wrong. Your task is to figure out which is which, and not to let them prove that they are smarter by putting you up on 'The Wall of Sheep'. ... But remember: not everybody is great at everything. You might be better than they are at X, and they might be better at Y. This is your chance to learn more about Y."

"And finally, just a couple of tips to help you get the most out of the conference:

• Have a back-up talk selected just in case you arrive at your first choice and find it is full. That *will* happen.

• Figure out which rooms are the biggest, and check out which talks are being presented in them. The organizers usually assign the hottest talks to the biggest rooms.

"Questions? ... If not here, you can catch me in the office. And remember that the burner phones can't go in the enclosure. They have to go in the lockers. Be sure to put your real phone on top, screen up."

There weren't any questions after lunch either. That's what you get when you work with a bunch of really smart, self-confident people.

The Bears, however, kept us entertained that afternoon. It was Igor's turn to make the weekly courier run over to the Центр (Center) as they called it. When he came back, there was a big double-wrapped envelope in the pouch hand-cuffed to his left wrist.

"EYES ONLY for you, Sasha," said Igor. "Sign here."

"Damn!" said Sasha. "It's that psycho Targeting Officer again. … It's a list of eAddresses for provincial Democratic and Republican Party organizations that he wants us to target to establish a foothold for an upcoming operation."

"Natasha, you take the Democrats, and Boris, you take the Republicans."

"Let's just send them all *Office Monkeys*," said Boris. "That doesn't need a lot of prep, and it always gets some hits."

"I guess if I can tell him 'established X number of footholds, as per your instructions,' that will be enough," said Sasha.

"Brevity in one's reporting is the hallmark of an insightful analyst," replied Natasha.

The Bears kludged together a phishing expedition and got it out the door by CoB Moscow.

I sent out the requisite situation report:

IMMEDIATE
T O P S E C R E T SAVOY
LIM/DIS NOFORN
SUBJ: Incoming Cozy Bear Phishing Attack Against Regional Democratic and Republican Party Organizations

11MR15 14:14Z

Cozy Bear released a volley of 74 spear-phishing eMails addressed to recipients at various regional Democratic Party organizations, and 63 addressed to recipients at a selection of regional Republican Party organizations.

Targeting instructions that accompanied the lists of eAddresses said not to attempt to exploit any successful penetrations, but to establish a foothold in the victim systems in preparation for an upcoming operation.

Boris was right. We saw three hits on the *Office Monkeys* video before we went home for the evening. They were all from Eastern time. As the world turned and it got to be office hours in Central, Mountain, and Pacific time, more hits came in, but we didn't see those until we came in the next morning.

That morning, Sasha was pleased to be able to report to the Targeting Officer that the Bears had established eleven footholds in the victim systems as instructed. Such a quick response apparently satisfied the Targeting Officer, because we didn't hear any more about him from the Bears for the rest of the month.

A Big Contretemps

Floris was going bananas about the briefing for the Director that morning. He wanted everything to go right. That's why he was fishing for a way to get rid of me during the briefing.

"But the Director's office called to make sure that I'd be here for the briefing," I lied. I didn't think he'd call to check up on me, what with all the other things he was hiccupping about.

I don't know why he was so worried. It was just a dime-a-dozen dog and pony show that started with a meet-and-greet with the team. What could go wrong?

Floris' extended arm preceded the Director and his ADC into the shielded enclosure, pointing the way for them as he held the door open. The first person in the 'welcoming' line was Saskia, who stuck out her hand to shake the Director's, and said "Saskia Kortekaas," before Floris could catch up with the Director and get his mouth in gear.

I don't know which flummoxed the Director more. Saskia's directness, the working class Hague accent that she could put on when she wanted to for the effect, or the text of the T-shirt she was wearing. It said:

1f u c4n r34d 7h1s u r34lly n33d t0 g37 l41d

Must have been the accent. I was fairly sure that the Director couldn't understand her T-shirt.

Next in line was Sjoerd, who crushed the Director's hand in a vice-like grip. He had on a T-shirt that said:

A Black Hole is what happened
when God tried to divide by zero

It's a computer joke. Had hackers rolling in the isles at that conference the first time whatshisname said it.

Then came Menno, who's seen too many episodes of *The X-Files*. His T-shirt said:

The truth is out there.
Anybody got the URL?

By the time the Director got to me, he was clearly looking for a way out of this looney bin, and was giving his ADC the high-sign to remember some other appointment or think up some emergency so they could leave politely. He reached in the breast pocket of his suit coat and pulled out his cell phone.

Before Floris could introduce me, I said, "I'm afraid we're going to have to ask you to leave, sir. Cell phones are not allowed in the shielded enclosure. There is a sign on the door that warns everyone of this fact."

"You do know who I am?" asked the Director.

"Of course," I replied. "But that doesn't give you the right to compromise the security of this project by bringing a cell phone into the shielded enclosure."

"You're the American, aren't you?" said the Director. "I'll have you on a plane out of here tomorrow morning!"

"Where's that famous Dutch *bespreekbaarheid* (discussibility)? Shouldn't a little kid be able to tell the King that he has no clothes?"

The Director spun on his heel and was heading for the door, when I called after him.

"If you could come back the same time tomorrow, we can demonstrate why it is important that this rule apply to everybody," I said to his back.

That got his attention. He stopped, and turned around to face me. "Tomorrow?" he said. He turned to look at his ADC, who replied, "Yes, sir, tomorrow would be possible, but an hour later would be more convenient."

The Director nodded.

"For the demonstration, sir, we will need you to bring a cell phone, the same model as the one you are using. One that is working and can be used to make and receive phone calls. We don't want to compromise your real phone for the demonstration."

He looked pensive.

"We want you to supply the phone so that there can be no question as to whether we have had physical access to it before the demonstration."

His ADC made a note on his phone. I frowned at him.

"And we will need your ADC to accompany you. He is going to be your trusted observer of the attack on the test phone from the operational end, here in the shielded enclosure, while you and the phone are in an unclassified conference room outside."

"You seem pretty sure of yourself," said the Director.

"We do know what we're doing, no matter how bedraggled we look."

"Why tomorrow and not right now?"

"You'll need time to get a demonstration phone, and we'll need time to set up the attack," I replied. "And, by the way, please have whoever sets up the phone include a list of fictitious contacts with phone numbers. We'll 'exfiltrate' them as part of the demonstration."

As they were leaving, I heard the ADC say, "Speaks pretty good Dutch for an American, wouldn't you agree, sir?"

The next morning, the Director showed up on time with his ADC, who had the test phone.

"Good morning, sir," I said to the Director. "Please have a seat. The demonstration will take about fifteen minutes. Would you like a cup of coffee?"

Offering the Dutch a cup of coffee when people come in is practically obligatory in Holland. Not offering one would be a huge social faux pas. An American friend of ours once went to Holland to visit the family of the Dutch high-school student they had hosted. When he came back, he proudly announced: "I learned the Dutch word for 'Hello'! It's *Coffee?*" And, in a way, he was absolutely right. The first thing the Dutch say when you come into the house to visit is "*Coffee?*". Even the guy who comes to fix the washing machine gets greeted like that.

Simon had a cup of coffee and the ubiquitous cookie that goes with it in front of the Director before he could say 'yes'. It had just the right amount of milk and the kind of cookie that the Director preferred. We'd done our homework. We called his secretary and asked.

"If you would just put the test phone on the table, please, sir," I said to the ADC, "and your cell phone as well. Then, if you would be so kind as to follow Saskia, she will take you into the shielded enclosure so you can see the attack end of the demonstration."

"The phone on the table will ring in a minute or two, sir," I said to the Director. "No longer than it takes to walk to the shielded enclosure. If you would just pretend that it is your phone and answer the call."

"You're the one with a Dutch wife?" he asked.

"Yes, sir," I replied. "She and your wife studied together at Leiden."

That got his attention.

"They had lunch together last week in The Hague with a bunch of old school girlfriends."

"Yes," said the Director, " I seem to remember Caroline saying something about that."

The phone rang. The Director picked it up and looked at the screen.

"It says that the call is from Jan-Willem," said the Director.

The Director pressed the button to accept the call, and said, "This means that we're ready to start, Jan-Willem?"

But it wasn't the Director's ADC. He was seated next to Saskia in the shielded enclosure and his phone was on the table. We had spoofed his number into the Caller ID. The voice on the phone was Sjoerd's.

"Saskia, Saskia, it's all my fault, Saskia. It'll never happen again, Saskia, You've got to forgive me, Saskia! Here's a big bouquet of roses to say how sorry I am, Saskia."

An image of a lovely bouquet of roses appeared on the screen of the test phone.

"It's not Jan-Willem," said the Director to me, with a look of surprise on his face.

"Young man, you clearly have the wrong number," said the Director, and hung up.

The phone rang again before he could put it back down on the table. This time the Caller ID said it was his wife's cell. "Thanks, Kathy," I said to myself, hoping Kathy would receive the psychic vibrations. We've been married a long time. Sometimes it works. Of course Kathy had Caroline's cell number. They'd just had lunch last week.

"This is part of your demonstration, isn't it?" said the Director.

I put on my best poker face.

He hesitated for a moment, but let the call go to voicemail.

"The party you are calling is not available at the moment. Please leave a message at the beep," said the voicemail computer.

"The phone you are speaking from has just been pwned," said my voice to the voicemail computer. "Thank you for your attention."

"What do you think that you've proved?" asked the Director. "That you can spoof Caller ID?"

"We haven't proved anything yet," I replied. "The proof of the pudding will be in what your ADC just witnessed."

"You can bring him back in, Sas," I said into the emptiness of the conference room.

"What was that all about?" asked the Director. "Oh, you have the room bugged. Is that it?"

"Feel free to have a tech team come inspect the room," I said. "They won't find anything."

"More coffee, sir?" asked Simon.

The Director waved Simon off with a frown.

"They won't be a moment," I said to the Director. "They just need to collect the show-and-tell."

About a minute later, Saskia walked in with the Director's ADC, who was carrying a file folder, and a digital voice recorder.

"It's incredible, sir," said the ADC. "If I hadn't seen her do it with my own eyes, I'd never have believed it. Just take a look at this, sir," said the ADC, placing the file folder on the table in front of the Director and opening it to reveal a close-up color photo of the Director. "That's you, sir, checking the Caller ID of the second phone call, supposedly from your wife. It was taken by the camera on the test phone. The background of the photo is clearly recognizable as this conference room."

The Director was nonplussed.

"But there's more, sir," said the ADC, pressing 'Play' on the digital voice recorder.

"What do you think that you've proved? That you can spoof Caller ID?"

"We haven't proved anything yet. The proof of the pudding will be in what your ADC just witnessed."

"You can bring him back in, Sas."

"What was that all about? Oh, you have the room bugged. Is that it?"

"Feel free to have a tech team come inspect the room. They won't find anything."

"Jan-Willem," said the Director, "I want a tech team in here immediately to inspect this room for bugs."

"Of course, sir, but I think it will prove a waste of time and resources," said the ADC, turning over the photo of the Director looking into the phone camera, to reveal a print-out of the fictitious address book from the demo phone.

Contact	Phone Number
Sinterklaas	12345
Zwarte Piet	67890
Johannes Vermeer	13579
Johan van Oldenbarnevelt	24680
Suske en Wiske	14703

The Director picked up the demo phone and opened the address book. He stared at it for a minute, comparing the entries, and then said, "Turn this damn thing off before it compromises anything else!"

Simon picked up the phone, turned it off, and put it in a Faraday shield bag.

"We'll be happy to brief you without your cell phone anytime at your convenience, sir," said Floris with a smile.

The Director wasn't smiling. He stood up, but didn't move.

"Jan-Willem," he said to his ADC, "schedule a briefing with this lady and these gentlemen at their convenience. I think I'd like at least an hour of their time."

The next morning when we came in, everybody's in-box had a memo that prohibited the possession of cell phones in any classified area. It was signed by the Director.

The RNC Hack

Spring was in the air. The tulips were blooming, and Kathy wanted me to take a weekday off so we could go to the Keukenhof Gardens to see the flowers. We had always wanted to go, but had never been in Holland when the flowers were in bloom, as if she had gone before we got married and she left Holland.

"You know that means we'll have to get up early if you want to avoid the crowds, even on a weekday," I said.

We decided on a Tuesday. Things had been slow at the office. It was almost as if the Bears were hibernating.

When I asked Floris for the day off, he said, "We were there last week. The theme this year is 'Vincent van Gogh'.

"They're celebrating the 125th Anniversary of his death," said Saskia, who was hanging around Floris' terminal when I walked up. "There's a portrait done in tulips."

I put those two comments together with the fact that Floris and Saskia were both off last Wednesday to conclude that the 'we' in Floris' comment equaled him and Saskia.

The brochure Kathy and I got at the entrance informed us that the gardens cover more than 80 acres packed with over seven million flowering plants, crisscrossed by fifteen kilometers of paths. That's a lot of paths, but we didn't walk them all. There's more than enough to see without wearing out your shoes. We did, however, take plenty of pictures and I think Kathy eMailed them all to our daughter that evening. She was still eMailing and posting to FaceBook when I called it an early night. She, conversely, was still asleep when I got up the next morning to go in to the office.

"You missed all the fun yesterday," said Floris when I got in. "Sasha came in — wearing a suit, can you imagine? — with a targeting list handed down from on-high. The powers that be want the Bears to hit the Republican National Committee."

The Bears spent Wednesday, Thursday, and Friday getting the spear-phishing attack on the RNC ready.

"Everybody got their spears ready?" asked Sasha half an hour before going-home time on Friday.

Boris was responsible for the 47 eMails that would carry the *Office Monkeys* ZIP file. "A golden oldie," he called it.

Natasha had 58 eMails that would accompany a supposed Donors List with a malicious macro in it. "It always pays to follow the money," said Natasha.

Igor's contribution was 39 eMails that would convoy a PDF with a malware payload entitled *The Dirt on (a named Democratic Party Presidential candidate)*. "That will awaken somebody's prurient political interests for sure," said Igor.

"That makes 144," said Sasha. "Let's lock and load."

"Ready."

"Ready."

"Ready," said the three Bears.

"Пуск! (Pusk!, Launch!)" said Sasha, and they closed up shop for the weekend.

The eMails went out from a compromised regional Republican organization eMail account in the Mid-West.

I sent out the obligatory situation report:

IMMEDIATE
T O P S E C R E T SAVOY
LIM/DIS NOFORN
SUBJ: Incoming Cozy Bear Phishing Attack Against the Republican National Committee
17AP15 14:12Z
Cozy Bear released a volley of 144 spear-phishing eMails addressed to recipients at the RNC. The eMails were dispatched from a compromised regional Republican organization.

We waited expectantly for the first returns to come in. We were still waiting at CoB, and not a data packet to be seen coming out of TOR from the RNC.

"Saskia, check the implant," said Floris.

"Implant reports all systems normal," said Saskia from 'The Watch'.

"Mark, is it a holiday in the States or something?" asked Floris.

"Not that I'm aware of," I replied. "If it was, the Bears would know as well or better than I."

"OK, let's close it up for the weekend," said Floris. "The Bears went home. Let's go home. Have a good one, everybody."

When we came back in on Monday, the folder for returns from the RNC phishing expedition on the Bears' server was still as empty as Old Mother Hubbard's cupboard.

The Bears were noticeably upset. Bear Chat had an endless list of system checks requested and completed.

"There's nothing wrong with our system," said Boris. "Time to bite the bullet and ask the guy who gave you the targeting list to confirm that the eAddresses are valid."

"You go ask him!" said Sasha.

"Not for an Order of Lenin presented by Lenin himself!" said Boris.

"Anybody got a better idea?" asked Sasha.

"Maybe," said Igor, "it's a filter that is blocking eMails with attachments and active links. I've read theoretical discussions of that kind of thing."

"I need something more than a 'maybe' to take to the Targeting Officer, or I might not live to regret it," replied Sasha.

"How about this?" said Natasha. "We pick one eAddress from each of our three lists, send these three eAddresses an eMail from the compromised account with no links and no attachments; just a nebulous question, like 'when will the (a named Republican Party Presidential candidate) campaign be holding its next event?'"

"What's that get us?" asked Sasha.

"If we get an answer to each of these eMails, then we can say with a reasonable amount of certainty that a spam/malware filter at the RNC probably ate the phish," replied Natasha, "because the eMails without links and attachments made it through and got answered."

"That sounds like something I might be able to sell to the Targeting Officer and get out alive. Let's give it a shot.

No, not a 'shot'. That sounds too much like the Targeting Officer. He's unreal. Let's give it a try."

"Would you buy that?" asked Floris.

"Sure," I said. "Remember that newsletter that came out of the Fort last month? There was this article from some Cyberwarfare wheel that said 90% of all the successful data exfiltrations and breaches that the Federal Government and Private Industry have suffered in the last five years were the result of spear-phishing attacks aimed at naïve employees."

"No, I must have missed it."

"With a success rate like that, why should the Bears spend their time and money on another approach? It's not like they have unlimited funds," I continued.

"Good point."

"The wheel bemoaned the inability of Americans not to click on a link or open a file," I said. "In his conclusion, he made the point that somebody should develop a system that would categorically prevent users from clicking links and opening unverified attachments, because it would make them a fortune."

"In other words, somebody is making a fortune off the RNC for providing them iron-clad phishing protection."

"That about sums it up," I said.

The Bears carefully crafted the nebulous eMail questions, but had to wait to send them so that the date-time stamps would match local working hours at the compromised account. And, of course, eMails with nebulous questions like the ones they asked don't get answered right away. Sasha and Boris hung around with a couple of bottles of export quality vodka after CoB Moscow, waiting for the replies. The first one didn't come in until just before our CoB. When we went home, Sasha, Boris and the vodka (what little was left of it) were still waiting for the other two.

When we came in Tuesday morning, the date-time stamps of the other two eMail replies showed that they were sent after the zero two hundred hour Moscow. The video motion detector on the hallway camera logged Sasha and Boris out at 02:47 Moscow. They both appeared to have balance problems as they staggered down the hall away from the camera. Neither of them was seen again until after lunch Moscow.

Sasha spent the rest of the day writing a report about the RNC attack. He had Boris and Igor and Natasha read it before he put it to bed to age overnight. Wednesday morning, he came in wearing a suit, picked up the report and went out, presumably to face the Targeting Officer who wanted them to do the RNC.

When he came back, he looked very relieved.

"They bought it!" he said. "We can forget the RNC. I brought champagne to celebrate!"

The Bears closed up shop early on Wednesday.

I sent a copy of Sasha's report on the RNC attack (along with a translation) back to the Fort.

I called my contact at the Fort on the opscom.

"Any idea who's doing the cybersecurity for the RNC?"

"None."

"Somebody ought to find out and take a look at how they make it work, using the excuse that we want to check for vulnerabilities that we, I mean the Bears, could exploit."

"That sounds like the kind of idea that cash awards are made of."

"Don't spend it all in one place," I replied. "You know good and well that if it was submitted over my name, it would go straight in the bit bucket."

"Thanks," he typed. "I'll get to work on it."

Over his signature, a suggestion like that would sail through.

The compromised regional Republican Party organization eMail account gave the Bears a foothold from which to send eMails with an authentic, verifiable 'reply to' address, but the info carried in the eMails accessible from this account was too boring to report.

"This stuff is a patentable cure for insomnia," said Boris who had been reading the eMails sailing back and forth between local Party members. I've seen the catering details for a 'big' event: they figured five gallons of iced tea and six dozen donuts. If everybody who comes only gets one donut—and who only eats one donut?—that's 72 attendees. That's not what I'd call 'big'."

"Another thread was about ordering print campaign materials for a local candidate," continued Boris. "The discussion centered on whether to use sixteen point for the headline, or would it be better to make it thirty-two point? They decided on thirty-two point, because that would mean less text on the poster, and they didn't have that much to say about the candidate when it came down to it."

"Then there was this really interesting commentary on the physiques of their constituency. The question was how many "Vote for (a named US Person)" T-shirts to buy. Looking at the number of T-shirts they decided to purchase in each size, I was struck by an invasive image of the elephantine proportions of their overfed petit bourgeois voter base. The order was for five small, a dozen medium, five dozen large, and a gross extra-large," said Boris, who normally wasn't the type to throw puns based on Communist political rhetoric around.

"The hottest thing I saw was an eMail exchange between two of the Party workers (each married to other people)," complained Boris, "who were conducting a love affair via their Party eMail accounts. I know there's a requirement for information that the Резидентура (Rezidentura)[15] can use for black mail, but I think the Резидент (Rezident) would question our sanity if we handed him the dirt on two low-level volunteers at such a rural Party organization."

I couldn't quite agree with Boris on the last one. I'd seen some successful, very productive recruitments of secretaries, chauffeurs, and cleaners, so it wasn't so much their low-level jobs, as much as it was the lack of interest that the Rezident would have in a rural Party organization.

I summarized Boris' evaluation of the target in a tech message.

---

[15] Translator's note: Резидентура (Rezidentura) is the term that the Russians use for the SVR (née KGB) office in an embassy, what the Americans call 'The Station'. The Резидент (Rezident) is the Russian equivalent of the American 'Chief of Station'.

ROUTINE
T O P S E C R E T SAVOY
LIM/DIS NOFORN
SUBJ: Cozy Bear Evaluation of Compromised Regional
Republican Party Organization eMail Account
22AP15 10:22Z

Cozy Bear's evaluation of the intelligence value of the
content of the eMail exchanges on the compromised
regional Republican Party organization eMail account is
'Nothing to Report'.

Cozy Bear Does The Pentagon

It was Friday the 17th, just before quitting time in Moscow that Cozy Bear launched its spear-phishing attack on the unclassified eMail network of the US Joint Chiefs of Staff at The Pentagon. They didn't need to hang around this time like they did with the attack against The State Department. The new tools they had developed in the meantime automated the key collection tasks. It wasn't quite 'fire and forget,' but it came close.

Sasha was the last one out the door. "Have a good weekend, Igor," he yelled down the hall, as he spun off the combination lock on their vault door. He checked the handle, tugged on the door, initialed the closer's log, and then walked down the hall out of the field of vision of the camera.

We, on the other hand, had two more hours to go in our workday, due to the time difference with Moscow. The first return from The Pentagon came in before Sasha disappeared from view. A Major, who thought he was opening a PDF on the situation in Ukraine from a friend of his at NATO Headquarters, had just let the Bears into the system. His address book was on the Cozy Bear server before he finished reading the twelve-page document that actually had originated in NATO. Cozy Bear had just modified it a little to make it a delivery vector.

The first Situation Report on the attack was out the door before the Major's wife eMailed to remind him that they were going out to dinner tonight, and would he, please, bring a bottle of wine as a hospitality present for the hosts, Colonel and Mrs. (a named US person). She thought that they would like a German white wine.

Menno started a pool for how long it would take The Pentagon to close the penetration down. By the time he got to me, all the short positions were gone. Sjoerd had 'before we come in on Monday.' That made sense. The Pentagon runs a 24-hour shop, and the Bears had been kicked out of the State servers in just over one day. Saskia had 'before CoB Wednesday'; I didn't give much for her chances, but I've been wrong about things like this before.

"I'm betting that they won't be any faster than The White House at Thanksgiving," she said, as she gave Menno her money.

Floris wasn't worried that he had 'before CoB Friday'. "Their new package is bleeding-edge 1337," said Floris, "they didn't name it Прятки (Pryatki, *Hide and Seek*) for nothing."

All that was left was 'more than a week,' which seemed like throwing my money away, but it was only €1, and I'd won The White House pool, so I said "what the heck," and let Menno have my money.

"I almost took 'more than a week'," said Floris, "but I just couldn't see it running past next Friday with us looking over the Bears' shoulders, and you pinging on the Fort to get things done. You will be pinging, even though you've got all *that* money riding on it?"

I decided not to dignify that remark with a response.

The second return for the Bears was from someone who obviously needed a little humor in his (or her) dull Friday morning, and clicked on the *Office Monkeys* video link. There were five solid returns before we sent "Follow-up Report #1," and called it quits for the weekend.

When we came in Monday morning, there weren't any data packets from The Pentagon with a date-time stamp after 18:04 Friday Washington local time.

Sjoerd went over to collect his prize money.

"Why don't you hold off on that, Sjoerd?" said Floris. "There's a timer in the package that tells it to only call home during the Washington day shift. Let's see what's going on at 15:00 Local first. Washington won't be open before that."

I dutifully churned out "Follow-up Report #2," to inform them that there had been no activity from the Cozy Bear Pentagon penetration since CoB Washington time on Friday, being sure to highlight the fact that there was a timer in the package that restricted its activity to Washington local day-shift duty hours.

At 14:37 Local (08:37 Washington time), Saskia was on 'The Watch' position. "Too bad, Sjoerd," she said. "I just saw a bunch of data packets from The Pentagon coming in for the Bears."

"The money's practically mine," said Menno, who had 'before CoB Tuesday'.

I was typing up "Follow-up Report #3," to say that the penetration had resumed activity, when I got an informal from my contact back at the Fort. It said, "Pentagon thanks you for your efforts. They identified an old vulnerability that had not been patched as the cause of the problem, and the patch has been applied."

I showed the message to Floris, who was making a new pot of coffee. That's what I liked about Floris, he wasn't afraid to muck in with the rest of us when it came to doing grunt work, like making coffee, taking out the burn bags, and sweeping the floor.

"Patch has been applied!" said Floris. "Who do they have running cybersecurity there, a bunch of kindergarteners? Saskia just said that she can see the data being exfiltrated from their system, so whatever patch they applied didn't do anything to the Bears' penetration."

"Sounds like a brass hat farting us off to me," I replied.

"What's that in plain Dutch?" asked Floris.

"A stuffed shirt telling us to go away and leave him alone," I said. "Let me see if I can find a way around him."

I got on the opscom to my contact at the Fort: "Please ask the respondent from The Pentagon who said that the vulnerability has been patched to confirm that it was the POBCAK vulnerability."

"What's that when it speaks English?" asked my contact, who was a good bureaucrat, but a terrible collector.

"It's a trick question. Just ask him."

About ten minutes later, the opscom typed out: "Pentagon confirms that the POBCAK vulnerability has indeed been patched."

"Great," I typed. "If he told you they patched it, that means the respondent doesn't know anything more about IT than how to spell it, if that. POBCAK is pretty standard IT slang. It means 'Problem Occurs Between Chair And Keyboard.' In other words, it is a human error and you can't patch those with a software update. This is a spear-phishing attack and all it takes is a 'one Delta ten Tango' to make it work."

"I should have stayed in bed," typed my contact. "Pissing contests with The Pentagon always end badly, and me calling the colonel who said that they had patched the POBCAK vulnerability an idiot will start one for sure."

"In that case, just bypass the colonel. Tell him since he can confirm patching the POBCAK vulnerability, we can say for sure it is his eMail system that is leaking bogons[16], because the patch for the POBCAK vulnerability changes their shape. The bogons we're seeing have the shape indicative of the patch, and since he's the only one who has installed the patch, it must be his system."

"Her system," said the opscom. "A pissing contest and an EEO complaint.[17]"

"Forget the EEO complaint. Tell her nice that she needs to call the sysadmin for her UNCLASS eMail system — assuming she knows who that is — and have the sysadmin install a bogon filter for the data being exfiltrated via port 80 to IP ██████████. Any competent sysadmin should be able to shut down the penetration with that info."

---

[16] Translator's note: A *bogon* is a *bogus data packet*. In IT jargon, *bogons* are generally data packets that have been forged for nefarious purposes. In hackish (hacker jargon) the word *bogon* is used in the sense of being incorrect, absurd, and useless.

[17] Translator's note: EEO is the abbreviation used in government jargon for *Equal Employment Opportunity*, the government's program for handling discrimination complaints.

"Am I supposed to understand any of this?"

"No, nor is the colonel, but if she passes on what I just told you, it will get the penetration fixed. All she's been doing so far is telling us that she thinks there's no problem, and that we're busybodies. This is the politest way to get her to do what I want."

The opscom stayed silent for the rest of the day.

"It must have caught laryngitis," said Floris, when I mentioned it to him.

"One of the well-known side effects of a turf-war infection," I replied.

The last thing I did before heading out the door to go home was send "Follow-up Report #4," to inform people that the Cozy Bear penetration of The Pentagon UNCLASS eMail system continued active as before.

Menno didn't win the pool on Tuesday, nor Saskia on Wednesday, or even Floris on Friday. I did (again).

"Don't spend it all in one place," said Menno, philosophically. "€12 doesn't go as far as it used to."

"Don't knock it, Menno," I said. "It's *patat met pindasaus* and *loempias*[18] for me and Kathy. That's living high on the hog in my neck of the woods."

The turf fight continued until one of the Senior Executive Service[19] wheels from the Fort got in a car and

---

[18] Translator note: *patat* (French Fries) *met* (with) *pindasaus* (Indonesian peanut-butter sauce) and *loempias* (Indonesian spring rolls), typical Dutch take-away fare.

[19] Translator's note: Members of the Senior Executive Service are roughly equivalent in rank to General Officers in the Armed Forces.

drove down to The Pentagon to show the Chairman of the Joint Chiefs a copy of an eMail that we had recovered from the Cozy Bear feed coming out of The Pentagon. It was one the Chairman had sent himself less than two hours ago. It could have been a more recent one, if it wasn't for the fact that it's a good hour's drive down to The Pentagon. The traffic is horrible that time of day.

The Joint Chiefs' eMail system went off the air for a whole day, but they got it fixed by CoB (Washington) Thursday.

Rumor had it that the she-colonel in charge of the Joint Chiefs' UNCLASS eMail system was reassigned to Fort Lost in the Woods to run the Commissary, but it was only a C-val rumor[20] at best. I hoped she liked it there. It wasn't called 'Fort Lost in the Woods' for nothing.

When he came in on Friday and found that they had lost access to The Pentagon, Sasha wasn't particularly displeased. "We had unlimited access for ten days before they caught us this time," he said on Bear Chat. "That's the kind of stuff that promotions, cash awards, and trips abroad are made of."

"We finally got 'em!" said Floris. "Not too sleazy for a low-budget operation like ours," he added. "The beer is on me. It's Belgian. It's in the bottom drawer of the second filing cabinet, Sjoerd."

Both we and the Bears caught up on paperwork for the rest of the day. Just another run-of-the-mill Friday on the

---

[20] Translator's note: A 'C-val rumor' is a rumor with a validity of 'C' on a scale of A to C, where 'A' is fact, 'B' is a probability, and 'C' is a possibility. The qualification 'D-val' is used colloquially by practitioners for something that is made up, eg. 'fake news'.

front lines of the Cyber Cold War: 90% paperwork, 2% luck, 3% sweat, and 10% dealing with Headquarters bureaucrats who have no place in our business. Dealing with bureaucrats counts double, but the suits who claim to run things can't seem to comprehend that.

Half an hour before Bear going-home time, Sasha launched a spear-phishing attack against the Democratic National Committee. The Bears had already reeled in three phish before they went home for the weekend.

I went over to my terminal and typed up the de rigueur situation report:

IMMEDIATE
T O P S E C R E T SAVOY
LIM/DIS NOFORN
SUBJ: Incoming Cozy Bear Phishing Attack Against the Democratic National Committee
31JL15 16:13Z
Cozy Bear released a volley of 133 spear-phishing eMails addressed to recipients at the DNC. The system has already been successfully compromised.
The phishing eMails were sent from compromised eMail accounts of various regional Democratic Party organizations.

Menno wasn't in to set up a pool on how long the penetration would run. He, Simon, and Saskia were on a plane headed for Black Hat and DEF CON in Las Vegas. Probably just as well. None of us would have been anywhere close to the right answer. We would have been thinking in days and weeks, but the DNC penetration ran almost exactly nine months.

Bright Light City

What we missed on that laid-back, 'catch-up the paperwork' Friday was that we were missing three Bears: Boris, Sergej, and Natasha hadn't been logged when they arrived in the morning, or checked out at night. If we had noticed, I would have been thinking about where they had gotten to all weekend, but we didn't notice, and I was looking at the back of my eyelids at 23:23 Local on Sunday when I got a call from Menno. I could tell it was him by the Caller ID.

"Heemehrgancy! Heemehrgancy! Everybody to get from street!" said Menno in response to my "You rang?"

"It's late, Menno, and you're being too subtle," I grumbled into the phone.

"It's a movie quote," said Menno.

"Once more. I'm still asleep," I replied.

"Heemehrgancy! Heemehrgancy! Everybody to get from street!" repeated Menno, in what I was by now conscious enough to recognize as Russian-accented English from the movie *The Russians Are Coming*.

"Let me guess," I said, trying to sound awake. "A Russian submarine sailed up The Strip, and the sailors from the sub are trying to clear the street so they can take over Las Vegas."

"You said I should only call this number in a work-related Heemehrgancy," said Menno, for whom it was only 14.23 Local.

"Yes, I do recall something like that. This better be a good one."

"Guess who was in the session I just left," said Menno.

"Let's see. If it's a Heemehrgancy, then it must be a Russian."

"Right."

"Someone you know?"

"And you know her, too."

"Natasha?"

"You must be clairvoyant."

"She was wearing a T-shirt that she got here. It says:

Certified Russian Hacker

"Well, she certainly is that," I said. "Is Boris with her?"

"Not that I've seen."

"Thanks. You're right. It's a Heemehrgancy, but I can't do anything about it until tomorrow. Don't invite her to go dancing with you, or out to dinner. I'll find out. ... And I'll tell Sylvia."

"Ha ... ha," replied Menno, with an obvious lack of humor.

"I'll send you an SMS when I get things rolling, and, no, I won't want you to do anything. Just have fun at the event. Learn stuff!"

"You can go back to sleep now," said Menno.

"Good night."

"Who was that?" asked Kathy.

"It was Menno. It's not this late in Las Vegas."

"Is he having fun?"

"I suppose so. This was work-related."

"'Don't invite her to dinner' is work-related?"

"He met a Russian we're interested in at work."

"Oh," said Kathy who'd been married to me long enough to know that what I had just said was a believable explanation.

We both turned over and went back to sleep. No counting sheep required.

There was no point in rushing into action. I couldn't accomplish anything until D.C. woke up. This was a job for the FBI, and my only conduit to them was via the Fort.

Floris and I had a short conference when I got in. Saskia had called him about the same time as Menno was talking to me. She'd seen Boris in the hall on his way to a session.

Sjoerd was at 'The Watch.' We went over, and Floris asked: "You missing any Bears this morning?"

"Yeah, how'd you know?" asked Sjoerd. "Boris, Sergej, and Natasha are AWOL[21], and I checked the log. They were not in on Friday either. You think they got purged?"

"Nope. I think they're reasonably safe," I replied.

---

[21] Translator's note: The abbreviation AWOL is military jargon for *Absent WithOut Leave*.

"They're at Black Hat in Las Vegas," said Floris. "We got calls from Saskia and Menno to report that they'd seen them, well, seen Boris and Natasha. We're just assuming that Sergej is there, too."

"Some people have all the luck," said Sjoerd. "Even the three Bears get to go to Las Vegas."

"I get the point," I said. "It's too early to be working on funding for next year. I want to use the trip reports from this year to help justify it. Just remember: there'll be three fewer names in the burn bag for next year. Your chances will be higher."

"I'll start packing when I go home tonight," said Sjoerd with his typical brand of irony, as subtle as a sledgehammer.

"Anything important going on with the Bears?" asked Floris, trying to redirect Sjoerd's attention elsewhere.

"They're up to their ears in eMails from the DNC penetration. Sasha's been complaining," said Sjoerd, pointing to the screen for Bear Chat.

The last line said: "Don't those people every delete anything from their inboxes!"

"That's the tenth time he's typed that since they opened," said Sjoerd.

IMMEDIATE
T O P S E C R E T SAVOY
LIM/DIS NOFORN
SUBJ: Cozy Bear Phishing Attack Against the
Democratic National Committee Follow-up #1
03AU15 07:43Z
The Cozy Bear penetration of the DNC was successful.
It has harvested so much material over the weekend
that Cozy Bear is complaining about not being able to

keep up with the volume of eMails that they have collected.

"Tell me again why we are not supposed to read any of the eMails from the DNC," said Sjoerd.

"It's the rules of the game that I have to play by," I replied. "The people at DNC are American citizens, and I can't target American citizens."

"OK, those may be your rules, but why do we have to abide by them?"

"That was part of the agreement with your Director that landed me on your doorstep, along with US funding, equipment, and access to tech training courses back at the Fort."

"I still don't get it. It was alright to read the stuff coming out of The State Department, The White House, and The Pentagon, so why is it different for the stuff from the DNC?"

"State, The White House, and The Pentagon are government organizations. We have to read their stuff to determine if the material is classified, and then to support the assessment of what damage has been done by having classified material exposed to the Russians."

"All I can report for the DNC is the fact of collection by the Bears, and anything the Bears report about the DNC, because that tells us what the Bears' reporting requirements are."

"In other words, DNC collection is going to be boring from our point of view."

"Sounds like you've got a pretty good grasp of the situation."

It being a Monday, I gave my contact at the Fort until 09:00 his local time before I called him on the opscom.

"We saw your DNC report," he typed, "but nobody quite knows how to deal with it, because it's a civilian organization."

"I'm sure you'll figure out something," I typed as reassuringly as I could by putting a smiley at the end of the line. "But I didn't call about that. I've got another problem that will be easier to deal with, that is, if liaison with the FBI will be easier."

"Hey, that's what we can do with the DNC. Tell the Bureau," he typed. "What's your problem?"

I explained about the three Bears at Black Hat.

"What we'd like is for the FBI to do a work-up on them. You know the kind of thing: full names, passport numbers, visas, port of entry, credit cards they are using, a look at any electronics they brought. You can have the desk analyst print off some photos of the three Bears from the files to help the FBI spot them."

"The FBI will want jpg-s of the photos," typed my contact. "The quality will be better than a fax of a print."

"Whatever works," I typed. "There is, however, a catch. The host says that you cannot tell the FBI how we know that the Bears are there, nor how we know who they are."

"Got it. 'A closely held source says that …' That's what we usually tell them when we can't tell them where it's from."

"Let me know what liaison says," I typed. "I've got to have something to keep me entertained. We can't read anything from the DNC collection, so knowing that the

Bureau is chasing the Bears around Bright Light City would give us something to smile about."

About an hour later, my contact called back.

"The Bureau says they'll pass it on to the local office, which already has a team at Black Hat. Jake said unofficially that he asked for a 'tally-ho' if they spot our Bears, but he can't guarantee anything. Officially, there will only be an after action report, and they'll put us on distro for it since we submitted a targeting request."

"Thanks," I typed. "By the time the local office opens, we'll be long gone. Could you leave us a note on the opscom if you get a 'tally-ho' so we won't be left in suspense until you open tomorrow?"

"Sure; if I get one."

On my way home, which means just after 08:00 in Las Vegas, I sent Menno an SMS that said: "The ball's rolling. Tell Sas and Siem when you see them."

About 10 minutes later, I got an SMS back. "At breakfast together. 3 Bears 2 tables away. No porridge 4 them. Bacon n eggs instead."

Trust Menno to know what the three bears in the fairy tale had for breakfast.

The next morning, I stopped by 'The Watch' to see what was going on in the Bear Lair.

"No wonder the Bears were able to get into the DNC server so easily," said Sjoerd. "One of the Bears' defensive checks for their implant turned up a malware package mining for digital currency. The DNC doesn't have any cybersecurity at all."

"You're making this up to make me feel good," I replied.

"Nope. The punch line is yet to come. Take a look at this," said Sjoerd, scrolling the Bear Chat screen back to an earlier exchange between Sasha and Igor.

"Igor," said Sasha, "That malware digital currency miner package on the DNC computer gave me an idea. You think you could craft me a 'smoke screen' to deploy in case one of the systems we are in runs a scan?"

"You mean a digital currency miner?"

"That's right."

"Sure," said Igor. "You want it to really work?"

"No, not all the time. I just want to be able to turn it on if needed so we could make the defenders think they had found the problem, and give us a chance to erase our tracks before they could figure it was our implant."

"Aha, so I should point the mined coins to somebody else's account so they can't trace them back to us?"

"Right. How about the North Koreans? They're everybody's flavor of the month for bad guys."

"ROTFLMAO," typed Igor. "OK, there's a bunch of ready-made stuff out there that I could package up. I'll work something up and get back to you."

When I got to my terminal, there was a 'tally-ho' on the opscom waiting for me. It's great when things work like they're supposed to.

The hardcopy (there was no softcopy) FBI report on the Three Bears in Las Vegas came to the Embassy in the pouch, with instructions to pass unopened to the AIVD. It took a week after landing at the Embassy to make it to Floris' desk. The FBI had done a good job.

Natasha Alexandrovna Marinina

Traveled on a personal (unofficial) passport issued 6 years ago in St. Petersburg.
Traveler last visited the USA on a student visa for the academic year 2009-2010.
Records Check shows that she was enrolled in a graduate Computer Science program at Carnegie Mellon University (Pittsburgh, PA).

Boris Konstantinovich Polevoj

Traveled on a personal (unofficial) passport issued 5 years ago in Moscow.
Traveler last visited the USA on a student visa for the academic year 2010-2011.
Records Check shows that he was enrolled in a graduate Computer Science program at Stanford University (Stanford, CA).

Sergej Anatolevich Rybakov

Traveled on a personal (unofficial) passport renewed this year in Moscow.
Records Check shows that the subject was previously in the USA on a student visa for academic year 2007-2008, when he was enrolled in a graduate Computer Science program at University of California — Berkeley (Berkeley, CA).

Visas were issued individually by Embassy Moscow.

All travelers listed Moscow State University (MGU) as their place of employment.

Local street addresses, eMail addresses, telephone numbers, passport and visa numbers, as well as full-face and profile photos of the travelers in Las Vegas are included in the individual attachments.

Conference participation and hotel bills for all three travelers were charged to the same corporate credit card, one registered to Moscow State University (MGU). This credit card has previously been used to pay for travel expenses for individuals known to be Russian Foreign Intelligence Service (Служба внешней разведки, Sluzhba vneshney razvedki, SVR) officers.

Travelers had no personal electronics of any kind, i.e. no cell phones, no tablets, no laptops. They took notes at conference sessions using pen and paper.

Travelers charged their meals to their hotel rooms.

Travelers paid for purchases from vendors in cash, using old bills, nothing larger than a twenty.

"Those are some pretty classy Computer Science universities they've been to," said Menno as he finished the report. "Of course, they can't compete with my American university: MIT."

"I went to the School of Hard Knocks," I replied. "My first computer used vacuum tubes and mechanical relays."

"I'd loved to have seen one of those," countered Menno.

"No, you wouldn't," I said. "It only had sixty-four 'K' of memory and it overflowed all the time. My cell phone has more capability than my first computer."

"Hey, sixty-four GB isn't that bad," responded Menno.

"No, it's not," I countered, "but my first computer only had sixty-four *kilo*-bites of memory."

"KB!" exclaimed Menno. "Claustrophobia-city."

Home Again

On her first day back after Black Hat/DEF CON, Saskia was wearing an 'official' DEF CON T-shirt. It said:

> I went to DEF CON 2015,
> but there was no official T-shirt.
> All I got were the passwords to
> your eMail, bank, and Twitter accounts.

Saskia brought all those who had stayed behind a souvenir T-shirt. It was a black shirt with white lettering. The text said:

```
.tshirt {
        font color: #000;
        background: #FFF;
        overflow: hidden;
}
```

On the one hand, a hacker's T-shirt—especially a black T-shirt—is a way of communicating the hacker's status to other hackers. A T-shirt you got at Black Hat or DEF CON yourself shows your hacker creds, as in 'been there, done that, and have the T-shirt to prove it.' Saskia's was the only genuine DEF CON T-shirt. The ones she brought back to give to the team were just hacker T-shirts that she'd bought from a vendor at Black Hat. Not the same thing at all.

The message on a hacker's T-shirt is often based on humor, which is an integral part of hacker culture, but it can also be an expression of anti-authoritarianism, and sometimes it is a combination of the two.

Saskia's souvenir T-shirt was a combination of the two.

The joke, for those who are not HTML literate, is that the code on the shirt defines a white shirt with black letters, while the actual shirt is just the opposite. #FFF is the hexadecimal color code for web-safe white, and #000 is the code for black. The command 'hidden' says that the shirt should be tucked into your pants, which, of course, nobody on the team would dream of doing while wearing the shirt at work. Everything the shirt said was the reverse of what the real shirt was. That was its anti-authoritarian punch line.

"Very Zen," said Sjoerd.

Simon had on an 'official' Black Hat T-shirt. The text wasn't fancy. It just said "Black Hat 2015" over the official Black Hat logo. You could only get those with your registration package. They weren't for sale at any vendor's stand.

Simon's souvenir T-shirt said:

Russian Hackers Made Me Do It

"I wonder if the Bears bought any of those," said Floris.

"Not that I saw," said Simon.

Menno was wearing a T-shirt worthy of his opinion of his coding skills. It said:

My Code Passed the Turing Test

His souvenir T-shirt for the rest of the office said:

C0m9ut3r Wh1s93r3r

"Right-onitude!" said Simon. "Where'd you get that? I didn't see any of those. I'd have bought some myself."

"In the vendors' hall, about three tables after you turned around to go get a beer."

"We had a great time, and we learned *a lot*," said Saskia.

"Simon wound up on the 'Wall of Sheep'," said Menno. "But none of the Bears did."

"Siem took his own cell phone," said Saskia.

"He said he wouldn't be caught dead with the burner phone you gave him," explained Menno.

Simon didn't say anything, but he did turn a bright shade of red.

Meanwhile back in the Bear Lair: On her first day back from Las Vegas, Natasha had on her official Black Hat T-shirt; the same one that Simon was wearing. It wasn't a total fashion disaster. Nobody would ever see them side by side with the same T-shirt on. Like Saskia, she had brought the stay-behinds souvenir T-shirts. Hers said:

Crazy Russian Hacker

That's the same one that Menno had seen her wearing at Black Hat. It was clearly popular with the Bears. Sasha took off the T-shirt that he'd worn to work, and put on Natasha's.

"You should have gone outside to change shirts!" said Natasha. "This isn't a strip club."

"Not something you've never seen before," said Sasha.

Natasha threw a coffee cup at him. Missed him by that much, as Maxwell Smart was wont to say.

Sergej had on his DEF CON T-shirt, the same one Saskia had. His souvenir T-shirts were a conspiracy theorist's dream. They showed an American 'I voted' logo above the text:

Russian Hackers
Vote Early and Often

Boris showed his finely attuned fashion sense by not wearing either of his 'official' T-shirts today, which would have made him clash with Natasha and Sergej. Instead, he had on a T-shirt with the text:

Keep Calm
and
Blame Russian Hackers

That text clearly struck a chord with all the Bears. They all wanted one, but Boris' was the only one in Moscow.

"Where'd you find that?" asked Natasha. "I didn't see it anywhere."

"It was in the distant corner of the vendors' hall," said Boris. "I kept on going after you stopped at the Carnegie Mellon booth to talk to someone you knew there. It was a long hike, but I'm glad I made it."

His souvenir T-shirt for the rest of the team said:

Russian Hackers
Ate My Homework

"Duty calls," said Sasha. "Natasha, time to demonstrate your 'crazy Russian' hacker skills, and hack your way through some of those eMails that built up from the DNC while you three were gone."

"The what?" asked Natasha.

"The Democratic National Committee," replied Sasha. "That is the attack we prepared in early July, before the Center said to do The Pentagon first. We lost The Pentagon, and launched the DNC attack the day you guys left. Those people at the DNC never throw anything away. There's so much that we haven't been able to keep up."

When I got back from lunch, Floris waved me over to his terminal.

"Natasha's not just a well-filled T-shirt. She's almost as sharp as Saskia. She's already gotten a couple of reports out on the material from the DNC penetration," said Floris, pointing at his screen.

СОВЕРШЕННО СЕКРЕТНО СОРОКА[22]

American Democratic Party Donor Machinations

Democratic National Committee Donors' List includes personal information about the donors, such as street address, eMail address, telephone number, credit card and Social Security number. The identifying information is needed to comply with American election finance reporting.

Party Fund Raisers at the Democratic National Committee are engaged in bluntly transactional exchanges with wealthy donors, offering seating proximity to PotUS at a state dinner at The White House for minimum donations of US$100,000. The larger the donation, the closer the donor will be seated to PotUS. For donors with even deeper pockets, ambassadorships and appointments to various Federal Boards and Commissions are on offer.

---

[22] Translator's note: Russian = T O P S E C R E T MAGPIE (СОРОКА).

Party Fund Raisers have extensive dossiers on potential donors that provide not only information on their wealth, but also on their interests, annoyances, and passions.

Analyst comment: The dossiers and the personal identifying information are unencrypted and Center may wish to see complete details which could be used to hijack their identities for disinformation purposes.

СОВЕРШЕННО СЕКРЕТНО СОРОКА

American Democratic Party Makes Secret Agreement on Finances with (a named US Person)

The American Democratic Party concluded a secret written agreement with Presidential Candidate (a named US person) that gives the candidate control over the Party's finances, strategy, and all the money raised by the 'Victory Fund'. The candidate's campaign is to have the right of refusal for nominations to the position of Party Communications Director, and the right to make final decisions on all the other staff. The Party is further required to consult the campaign on matters of the budget, data, analytics, and mailings.

The salient argument put forward in favor of signing the agreement was that the Party treasury was empty and that the candidate had already provided the Party with a US$2 million 'loan,' with the promise of more if the agreement was signed. The candidate also agrees to actively raise money for the 'Victory Fund', a legal construct that can accept larger donations than candidate's own campaign. The candidate's prominence and extensive Donor List suggest that the result will be an extensive inflow of funds.

Analyst's comment: The full text of the agreement is available. The potential for blackmail is considerable.

"Thirty minutes after they sent the second report, there was a request from the America Desk at the Center for the full text of the agreement," said Floris. "It requested the agreement 'in the original language,' as the requestor was fluent in English."

I did a quick translation of Natasha's two reports and got them out under the heading of:

Cozy Bear's Reporting from its Collection of DNC eMails Shows Russian Targeting Requirements.

Once I got the report out, I wandered over to the coffee pot to refill my cup, where I ran into Saskia telling war stories from Black Hat.

"I went to this great panel discussion," said Saskia. *"Beyond the Gender Gap: Empowering Women in Security*. It was in a small room that reflected the number of women in IT, and at Black Hat. Men make up over 90% of the people doing this job, and over 98% of the people at Black Hat. For one thing, women find it hard to get funding to go."

"I resent that," said Floris. "You were in the first group from here to go, weren't you?"

"Yes, but what was that based on?"

"It was pure chance, and your chances were as good as everybody else's."

"I wanted to go based on my job performance, not on how well I fill a T-shirt, or what kind of 'plumbing' I have, said Saskia, glaring at Floris a little more heatedly than I thought justified."

"If you hadn't been doing a good job," said Floris, digging the hole he was in deeper, "your name wouldn't have gone in the burn bag."

"Saskia," I said, trying to pour oil on troubled waters, "Floris had nothing to do with selecting who went. I drew the names, and it was Kathy's idea to hold a drawing." Unfortunately, Saskia was too busy scowling at Floris to listen to me.

My analytical instincts told me that I was missing something in this exchange between Saskia and Floris. I thought I detected a hint of sexual tension, but I wasn't sure.

"Natasha was at the panel, too," said Saskia, "She was one of the ones who stood up to share their stories of life in the 'trenches' of IT security. She hit the nail right on the head when she said that women want respect — as in keep your hands to yourself — along with credit — as in promotions and cash awards — for their work."

I decided that a tactical withdrawal was in order. This was clearly a private fight between Floris and Saskia. I made my way over to 'The Watch', where Menno had on a poker face that could have easily turned a pair into the winning hand for a high-stakes pot.

"You play much poker out in Vegas?" I asked, trying to start a little light conversation with an eye towards hearing something less controversial about Black Hat.

"No, no poker," replied Menno. "And I only hit the slots seven-dollars' worth, but I won ten. There was just too much other stuff to do."

"Good time?"

"Yeah," replied Menno. "I learned a lot."

That was a big admission for Menno.

"My favorite was the *Advanced Practical Social Engineering* course," continued Menno. "Not just demos, but a lot of hands-on stuff. It was taught by the guy who wrote *Social Engineering: The Art of Human Hacking*. It was lots of fun. I kept wanting to talk about how the Bears do it, but I restrained myself. There were a lot of things in the course that the Bears could use. Luckily, none of them attended. I did, however, see Sergej at the *Arsenal* presentation of what they billed as a *High-Precision Social Engineering Tool*. They claimed it could run tailor-made social engineering campaigns with a high ratio of success. The demo looked promising."

Before Menno could continue, the audio from the Bears called out for his (and my) attention.

"I went to a great panel discussion entitled *Beyond the Gender Gap: Empowering Women in Security*," said Natasha. "The size of the room they stuck it in reflected the ratio of women to men in IT. It was the smallest room for any of the sessions I attended. The members of the panel made the point that men make up over 90% of the people doing this job, and over 98% of the people at Black Hat. The panel members were some of the top women in IT security. They shared their own experiences of getting to where they were."

"What? Tight T-shirts and loose jeans?" said Sasha.

"That's exactly what they were talking about," replied Natasha whose voice had suddenly taken on the 'friendly' whine of a buzz saw. "Women want respect—as in keep your hands to yourself—in addition to credit—as in promotions and cash awards—for their work."

"When they opened the floor to discussion, there was a Dutch woman who stood right up to share the story of life in her office, too," said Natasha, "She hit the nail right on the

119

head when she said that women want to be appreciated because of their job performance, not on how well they fill a T-shirt, or what kind of 'plumbing' they have."

"That must have been some panel," said Menno. "Glad I wasn't there. They'd probably have garroted me with a USB cable. Saskia makes hostile noises if I say something that isn't a hundred-percent gender neutral about coding. Sometimes she even complains if I hold the door open for her, or give her a pat on the back."

"Saskia was the Dutch woman' who Natasha was talking about," I warned. "I just left Saskia telling Floris about this panel in much the same tone of voice as Natasha. She and Natasha quoted each other."

"Whatcha think? Should I let Saskia hear this?"

"On the one hand, I think Saskia would be pleased to hear it, but on the other, she might want Floris to hear it to rub his nose in it, and that could be problematic," I said. "But telling her before you tell Floris would, I think, be the best order to do it in. Less chance of fallout for you that way."

"Make it so," replied Menno, doing his (in)famous imitation of Captain Picard's signature line.

Cozy Bear Counter-hacked by CIA

The Bears were getting bored with the DNC implant (and they weren't the only ones). It ran like a well-oiled machine, pumping out low-level political intrigues from the Democratic Party machine. It paid the rent, but it wasn't exciting, nor was it the stuff of promotions and more funding for billets and equipment.

"Weren't some of those addresses that we harvested from The State Department and The White House for people at CIA?" asked Sasha.

"Yes," replied Natasha. "Thirty-seven by my count."

"That might be enough," mused Sasha.

"Enough for what?" asked Boris.

"A phishing expedition," said Sasha.

"Against the CIA?" exclaimed Boris. "Less chance than Trotsky had in Mexico."

"What have we got to lose? Hackers of the World unite! You have nothing to lose but your boredom," retorted Sasha, who had obviously read too much Marx in his youth.

Despite objections from Boris, Igor, Evgenij, Sergej, and Natasha, Sasha got his way, because he was the Boss (Вождь, Vozhd').

They spent the next three days crafting the lures and the cover eMails that would take them to the thirty-seven eAddresses at CIA. The 'reply to' addresses would make them look like they came from State or The White House, but since the Bears no longer had a foothold at either of those places, the 'reply to' addresses would need to be spoofed.

"That's neither elegant, nor good tradecraft," complained Natasha on Bear Chat when Sasha made this pronouncement.

The Bears launched their CIA phishing attack at CoB Moscow time on Thursday.

"Почтальон (Postman) is running," said Boris on Bear Chat.

The Bears had learned not to send all their phishing eMails at once, because a common send-time was a giveaway that they were phish. The Bears, more precisely Natasha, had whipped together a little program that she called "Postman". It sent the phishing eMails out one at a time at random intervals to make them seem more legitimate.

"Those whom the gods wish to destroy get sent an eMail with a Trojan Horse," said Sasha.

"Euripides must be spinning in his grave," said Menno.

Sasha closed the vault door, spun off the dial of the combination lock, initialed the closer's sheet, and walked down the hall out of sight with dreams of a CIA hack and promotion dancing in his head.

I sent off an OPS IMMEDIATE situation report alerting the Fort to the attack.

IMMEDIATE
T O P S E C R E T SAVOY
LIM/DIS NOFORN
SUBJ: Incoming Cozy Bear Phishing Attack Against CIA
10SE15 14:12Z
Cozy Bear released a volley of 37 spear-phishing eMails
addressed to recipients at CIA.

Ten minutes later, Menno reported: "Incoming encrypted packets from TOR."

"It's a log-in screen for 'The Classified System'," said Menno.

The Bears' automated exploitation bot took over, and entered the password: password.

"Please make a selection," said the new screen, showing a list of choices.

The exploitation bot took the top item on the list: "Current Intelligence Reports."

"This is too weird," said Menno. "The bot's first guess at a password works, and the password is password, which is stupidosity in and of itself. This is the CIA!? What's wrong with this picture?"

Floris, Saskia, and I converged on 'The Watch' almost simultaneously to look over Menno's shoulder.

Saskia only needed 30 seconds to see what it was.

"It's a 'bomb'," said Saskia. "Shut down the implant before the bot can make another choice and trigger it."

"What?" said Menno, Floris and I simultaneously.

"It's a 'bomb'," repeated Saskia. "I saw it demo-ed at DEF CON. It is an aggressive counter attack to use against hackers. The counter-attacking computer will erase every disk connected to the host that is trying to pwn it. Shut down our implant, or the counter-attack program will follow the implant's connection to us and wipe all our disks!"

Menno was typing commands to the implant before Floris could say anything, as if he needed to.

The screens at 'The Watch' went dark.

"In its current form, the counter attack is aimed at automated bot hacks," said Saskia. "The giveaway to a real person should be that the first password you guess works. Like the gal doing the demo said: 'That never happens in real life'. The program is set to accept any string of characters shorter then 64 as the 'password'."

"I know I've complained about being two hours behind Moscow before, but I'll never do it again," said Floris. "That two-hour difference is what saved us this time."

"And having a real person on 'The Watch'," I said, conscious of Menno's scowl when Floris ignored him and gave the credit to the time difference. You have to treat the people on your team right. They are the ones who defend the thin line that separates success from failure.

"How long before it's safe to check to see if we can re-establish contact with the implant?" asked Floris.

"Three or four days at least," said Saskia. "The counter attack will check the connection every thirty minutes and will erase everything all over again if it gets contact."

"That goes way beyond just bearing a grudge," said Menno.

"In my day, we'd have called that a 'scorched earth' policy," I said.

"The Bears will have to figure out the re-wipe cycle, then boot to safe mode with no connections to the outside world. In the end, they'll have to get a new IP address," said Saskia. "Natasha was at the demo. Maybe she'll figure it out sooner."

"Maybe I could just ask politely for the CIA to shut their attack down, because it is interfering with our collection," I suggested.

"You think they'd agree?" asked Floris.

"If I ask 'pretty please' and point out how useful this access was when the Bears tried to get a foothold at State and The White House. The problem is how do I identify the Bears to the CIA to get them to turn off the 'scorched server' counter attack. I'm sure that this is not the only hack attack they've repulsed today."

"The gal doing the demo told us that by the time the fake 'log-in' screen reaches the attacking computer, the defending computer already has its network adapter settings, trace routes, and IP address, so I'd guess that you just tell them to turn off the attack against the Bears' IP address."

I fired up the opscom to my contact at the Fort and explained the problem to him.

"I'll get on to liaison, and see what I can do for you," he said. "If they balk, I can probably find some senior-level support for your 'request'."

He called back an hour later.

"I was able to make the case myself, without calling in any big guns," typed my contact. "Showing them your report on the initiation of the attack helped a lot. Liaison claims to have confirmation that they have shut down the counter attack against the Bears' IP, but I'd err on the side of caution before restoring contact with your implant. There might be some delay between confirming the shut down and it actually taking place."

I printed off the opscom response and took it over to Floris.

"That makes sense," he said. "Tomorrow morning should be soon enough."

"How about tomorrow afternoon," I countered.

"Not a lot of faith in your 'friends' at the CIA I see," said Floris.

"Not a lot of faith in D.C. in general," I replied.

"Liberal time off policy in effect for tomorrow," said Floris on the project chat circuit.

On Friday, I came in to the office after an unhurried lunch with Kathy, just in time to see Menno being dropped off by a stunning redhead in a Porsche whom I assumed to be Sylvia. Floris was still working the combination on the vault door when we walked up to put our cell phones in the lockers outside.

"This is it," said Floris. "Everybody else took the whole day off."

We all trooped over to 'The Watch' position together. No stopping to start that first pot of coffee, which is what would have happened on any normal day. This was the moment of truth.

Menno shut down all the comms ports except the one that he needed to talk with the implant.

"If there's going to be blow-back from the CIA 'scorched server' attack, it will stop with this terminal, and the rest of the project computers will be OK," said Menno.

Menno typed in a command, and the screens on 'The Watch' came to life. The video screen showed the empty hallway on the right. Bear Chat on the left picked up in mid-sentence with: "… any more problems with the reboot?"

"Looks like they had some problems restoring service this morning," said Floris. "Good thing we waited until after lunch to check on our implant."

"I see data coming out of TOR from the DNC," said Menno. "That looks pretty normal."

"I'm getting data from the Democratic Party implant," said Boris, "and it's decrypting OK."

"About (expletive) time," said Sasha.

"I told you it wasn't a good idea to try and phish the CIA," said Natasha. "But would you listen?"

"Shut up and see how much data we lost," said Sasha.

I walked over to my terminal to report that we had restored collection, but there was an opscom message alert from after we had gone home last night.

"Liaison requests that your follow-up report on the Cozy Bear phishing attack against the folks across the river just say that it failed, period. Nothing else," said the message. "Their counter attack capability is closely held, and knowledge of it would get too much distro, if you said what really happened in your report series."

That wasn't really a 'request'. It was the reason that liaison had given in so quickly when we asked to have the counter attack shut down. A credible source (that's us) could see what they were up to, and they wanted the source to keep its mouth shut: tit for tat.

I explained the situation to Floris, and he agreed (reluctantly) that we should keep our mouths shut for the good of the mission.

"I can't promise anything," I said, "but the horse trading isn't over yet. I'll let you know when it is."

An hour later when my contact at the Fort would be in, I fired up the opscom.

"We resumed collection about an hour ago," I typed. "That is to say that the collection that we didn't lose last night continues as before."

"Some people back here were holding their breath to see how you'd react to liaison's 'request'. They were talking about calling you back in to work so they could speak with you on the secure phone, but nobody could figure out how to do it."

"Good thing they didn't," I replied. "That would have raised a lot of questions here and brought the matter to the attention of senior people who are thus far unaware of it. Things are always settled much more easily, I think, when you keep the brass out of it. ... Now about the rejection of my request for funding for three travelers from the project to attend Black Hat/DEF CON in 2016? We were only saved from the Agency's 'scorched server' counter attack because one of the team here was at DEF CON on our dime this summer, where she saw the counter attack demo-ed, and could warn us off."

Just before CoB, I got a formal approval message for the trip with a full funding cite. I printed out the funding commitment just in case it got 'disappeared' from the message list, after which I sent:

IMMEDIATE
T O P S E C R E T SAVOY
LIM/DIS NOFORN
SUBJ: Incoming Cozy Bear Phishing Attack Against CIA
Follow-up #1 and final
11SE15 12:22Z
The Cozy Bear Phishing Attack against CIA initiated on
10 September failed.

I could almost hear the sigh of relief back at the Fort and across the river when I clicked 'Send'.

Floris was really pleased with the funding for Black Hat/DEF CON, even more so when I drew his name out of the burn bag as one of the three to go next year.

A Delicate Problem

It was one of those 'Winnie the Pooh' Wednesdays; the kind that happen from time to time to remind you of the rhyme by the bear of very little brain:

> On Wednesday, when the sky is blue,
> And I have nothing else to do,
> I sometimes wonder if it's true,
> That Wednesday is a workday, too.

Before I could finish the rhyme, however, Menno came over with a worried look on his face, which was unusual for the normally unflappable Menno. That held out hope of something exciting to keep me occupied for the rest of the day.

"I've got a delicate problem, Mark," said Menno, "and you're the only person I that can think of who might be able to get me out of it."

"I won't tell Sylvia that you were with us last night; I won't loan you money, and I can't prevent you from being extradited to the States."

"None of the above," said Menno, with a smile on his face that collapsed when he started telling me about his real problem.

"Sylvia got a new app for her phone," said Menno. "It's an ovulation tracker."

"Congratulations," I replied, hoping that congratulations were in order. Menno had never said anything about wanting to have kids before. "I'll get him or her a teddy bear, and Kathy can knit you a pair of booties or something."

"Yeah, thanks," said Menno, "but that's not it."

A flash of insight told me not to say anything so that he could get to the point.

"It's the app. I hacked it. I can see all the data she's got on it. You know, the kind of stuff: last time we had sex, the position we used, basal temperature, cervical mucus, onset of her last period."

"And you hacked the app?"

"Yeah. It was easy," said Menno. "There's a way to allow your partner to access your data, so you'll both be fully informed. As long as the account isn't already linked with a partner's account, anybody who knows her eMail address can link to her account. She doesn't have to acknowledge or approve the link. The first link request is automatically approved, no matter who made it: a creepy stalker, an obsessive ex, or the love of her life."

"That's not real smart security. Who did they have do this? Coke kiddies?"

"Maybe. They'll let anybody write code these days; intelligence is not a requirement."

"That's what keeps us in business, isn't it?"

"Yes," said Menno. "But that's not *my problem*. I tested the hack to make sure it wasn't a fluke."

"Good protocol. How?"

"I tried all the eMail addresses I know for women of childbearing age. I got two hits: my sister and Saskia."

"OK, looks like that proves it's not a fluke. So what's the problem?"

"How do I tell them that I hacked their accounts, and that I know they're both pregnant?"

"That's a problem! Saskia punches above the weight of a guy her size, and she'd slug you good."

"Don't I know it."

"Your sister?"

"She might never speak to me again."

"At least you wouldn't be black and blue squared."

"I'd like to avoid black and blue to any power, and I'd kind of like to have my sister speaking to me."

"Aha, so what you need is a plan worthy of the situation."

"Exactly, and since you seem to have an inexhaustible supply of them, that's why I thought you could help."

"Don't tell them."

"I'd like something a little more cunning than that."

"Has Sylvia deleted the app?"

"Yes."

"Have Sylvia call them and tell them about the vulnerability, but not about the proof that it's not a fluke. You did, I hope, have the good sense *not* to tell Sylvia about the proof?"

"No, I didn't tell her about the proof. My sister recommended the app to Sylvia, so that makes sense, but Sylvia doesn't know Saskia that well."

"OK, that takes care of your sister. How about we tell Saskia that I got an informal tip via a back channel about the vulnerability, and I want her to check the eMail address that we have for Natasha from Black Hat," I said. "I could say that we want her to do it because she'll understand any data we get from the hack better, because she's a woman."

"Make it so," said Menno.

"By the way, out of prurient curiosity, who's the father of Saskia's baby?"

"Floris, the night before we left for Black Hat," replied Menno. "She hasn't entered any sex in the app since then."

"That long? She's been doing a good job of hiding her morning sickness, and she's not showing. I wonder if Floris knows?"

"Maybe not. The app shows that she only just found out on Saturday. One of those DIY pregnancy tests."

"Man, that's a pretty complete data set on the app. No, I don't want to know any more. Floris and Saskia! I can't picture them as a couple."

I waited until after lunch to pitch Floris with the idea of having Saskia try the hack on Natasha's pregnancy app. I didn't want him to suspect any connection between my confab with Menno and the pregnancy app vulnerability. He only bought in on it after I pointed out that we could spoof a Russian telephone number onto the test phone we got for Saskia to try it with. The head he's got on his shoulders is there to do something more than keep his ears a respectable distance apart. Unfortunately, he only has IQ intelligence, and not Emotional intelligence.

Floris and I went over to give the task to Saskia.

"Yes, that sounds like it could work," said Saskia. "Natasha is technically very savvy, and very Western oriented. She might be using the app. I'm using it myself, but won't be after I get my hands on my phone," she said as she got up to go out to the cell phone locker outside the enclosure to delete the app.

Saskia's face hadn't given anything away when I told her about the vulnerability, but I hear that she's not a girl to play poker with.

Floris, however, had a puzzled look on his face when Saskia said she was using the app. If I hadn't known what Menno told me about the info on Saskia's app, I'd probably have had a puzzled look, too. But I did know, and I was sizing Floris up.

"He definitely doesn't know," I said to Menno after the conference with Floris and Saskia.

"Somebody has got to tell Floris," replied Menno.

"No, you mean that Saskia has got to tell Floris," I said. "It's her 'secret', and we *officially* know nothing. If you tell Floris, you have to be able to explain how you know, and you're right back at square one: the black and blue square to be precise."

"That's a basic 'geometric' way of focusing on the essence of the matter," said Menno. "I think I'll keep my mouth shut."

"Keep in mind," I said, "that this secret has a 'use by date', which is somewhere around the time that she can't fit in her jeans anymore, even by leaving the top button undone. After that, her condition won't be a secret from anyone."

It took a couple of days to get the phone we needed to try and hack Natasha's ovulation tracker app, but she either wasn't using it, or wasn't using it with the eAddress we had for her. At least we got Saskia off the buggy app without getting Menno beat to a pulp.

The 'use by' date of Saskia's secret turned out to be the day before Halloween, which was a Friday. Saskia came in in an 'expectant mother' costume and told Floris "Trick or Treat." A heated exchange of recriminations followed, finishing with a one-two sucker punch that left Floris out of breath and on the floor with a black eye.

"See? I told you she punches above her weight," I said to Menno.

Menno and I got Floris vertical, and rolled him down to the med center in a desk chair. When the duty nurse came out, he explained that he hadn't been watching where he was going, had tripped over a chair and hit a desk with his eye before landing on the floor.

The nurse looked at Menno and me skeptically.

"It's his injury," I said in reply to her unspoken question. "We are just the ones who picked him up and helped him down here."

"I want to keep him here to see if he has a concussion," said the nurse.

Menno and I went back to the shielded enclosure, where we found Saskia on 'The Watch'.

"You should give him points for gallantry," I said. "He said the black eye was an accident."

"I'll give him another accident, if he doesn't leave me alone," replied Saskia with a look that would stop a charging rhino in its tracks. "I'm going to be a BOM mother[23]. That's what I'm going to do."

The nurse called to say that Floris did not have a concussion, but she'd sent him home to convalesce.

"I wonder if the desk that hit him needs any medical attention?" asked the nurse.

"She doesn't seem to," I said.

"She?" queried the nurse.

"Sorry," I replied. "As you may have noticed Dutch isn't my native language. I must have used the wrong pronoun."

"Sure you did," said the nurse with a hint of irony in her voice. "Just tell her that if she wants to talk, she can come see me."

I passed on her message, but Saskia just kept sitting at 'The Watch' with the headphones on, listening to the Bears who weren't saying anything.

About an hour before going-home time Moscow, Sasha sent Boris a message on Bear Chat.

"How are those HVAC phishing spears coming?" typed Sasha.

"I've got 127 ready to go, and should have another 5 by CoB," replied Boris.

Menno called me over to 'The Watch'. He'd taken over from Saskia, who was now reviewing the code for the new persistence subroutine that Igor was working on. There was

---

[23] Translator's note: A *BOM Mother* is a very Dutch feminist concept. The abbreviation *BOM* stands for *Bewust Ongehuwde Moeder* (*Purposely Unwed Mother*)

a bug in it, and Igor couldn't find it. My money was on Saskia to find it before Igor.

"OK," said Menno, pointing to the exchange on Bear Chat. "I've looked up the abbreviation HVAC in Russian and English, and none of the expansions I'm seeing make any sense to me."

"You remember the big hack of the payment systems for the American retail chain store Target early last year?"

"Nope."

"The point of entry for the hack was via the Internet-connected Heating, Ventilation and Air Conditioning control system, that's HVAC in alphabet soup."

"You're kidding."

"No, I'm serious. The intruder stole some login credentials from the outside contractor that provided Target with HVAC services, and used those credentials to gain a foothold on the company's payment systems. The original hack of the contractor's system was via a spear-phishing attack run by the intruder a couple of months before the penetration of Target's payment system was discovered."

"Oh, I get it. The HVAC contractor isn't worried about IT security, because they figure no one is going to mess with that, because there's no money in it, and no secrets to be had."

"It took folks a while to figure out that the attack had come via the HVAC," I said. "What people still don't get is that you can weaponize this kind of hack. Just imagine what would happen if someone hacked the HVAC here or at the Bear Lair, and simply turned off the cooling system."

"We'd have to turn all the computers off, because without the cooling system they would overheat and fail one by one. We'd be out of business. No wonder the Bears are interested in it."

"So give me a heads-up when they launch," I said. "I'll want the list of eAddresses so I can report who the targets are."

"That's bleeding-edge l337," said Menno. "You have been round the block three or four times."

IMMEDIATE

T O P S E C R E T SAVOY

LIM/DIS NOFORN

SUBJ: Incoming Cozy Bear Phishing Attack Against HVAC Control System at US Governmental Organizations

30OC15 15:17Z

Cozy Bear released a volley of 132 spear-phishing eMails to addressees who have access to the control systems for the Heating, Ventilation and Air Conditioning (HVAC) at six US Governmental Organizations.

The HVAC systems under attack are:

The White House

The House Office Buildings

The Senate Office Buildings

The State Department

The Pentagon

The FBI Office Building.

Floris and Saskia

Monday morning we came in to find that all six of the phishing targets had bitten on the lures, and that the Bears were playing with the temperature settings at The State Department. I dutifully called up a situation report blank and started typing.

IMMEDIATE

T O P S E C R E T SAVOY

LIM/DIS NOFORN

SUBJ: Incoming Cozy Bear Phishing Attack Against HVAC Control System at US Governmental Organizations Follow-up #1

02NO15 08:37Z

Cozy Bear has gained a foothold in all six of the targeted governmental Heating, Ventilation and Air Conditioning (HVAC) systems.

The HVAC systems under Cozy Bear control are:

The White House

The House Office Buildings

The Senate Office Buildings

The State Department

The Pentagon

The FBI Office Building.

Cozy Bear is at present adjusting the temperature settings in the Main State office building.

Command and control communications from Cozy Bear to the target HVAC systems is via port TCP:█ (HTTPS).

The icy chill between Floris and Saskia hung in the air of the shielded enclosure like an iceberg hunting for the Titanic. I wished I could figure out a way to turn up the heat between them, so I called Menno and Sjoerd over for a conference to discuss the problem.

"You're the one with all kinds of cunning plans," said Menno. "You go and talk to *him*."

"I second that motion," said Sjoerd.

"Two against one," I replied. "That's not fair."

"Fair or not, you're the one with the best chance of achieving a reasonable semblance of an armistice," said Menno.

"My parents would *never* approve of Sas," said Floris. "Father knows the Director."

"So, what's the Director going to tell your father about Saskia?" I replied. "Pleasant young woman. Dressed in jeans and a T-shirt like all of them down in your son's shop, but sharp as a tack. She hacked my cell phone in less than fifteen minutes with my ADC watching over her shoulder. He was smitten with her. ... Did I get the tone right?"

"Yes, that sounds like the way he and father talk."

"Knows the Director?" I mused out loud. "Kathy knows the Director's wife. Maybe she knows your mother? What's your mother's name?"

"Trien," said Floris.

"I don't recall Kathy mentioning her, but I'll check," I said. "In the meantime, buy Saskia some flowers and apologize."

"I bought her flowers, and she hit me with them."

Menno called me over to 'The Watch'.

"I don't get it," said Menno. "The implant in the HVAC controller at State just went off the air, and Sasha is happy."

"They found it!" typed Sasha. "Igor, you're a genius!"

"I expected you'd be learning new Russian curse words when the implants shut down," I said. "I don't think we're in Kansas anymore."

"Kansas?" said Menno. "Is that the name of some powershell[24]?"

"No, it's a movie quote," I replied. "From *The Wizard of Oz*. A little girl and her dog living in the US state of Kansas get picked up by a tornado and they come down in a magical land. She takes a look around and says: 'I don't think we're in Kansas anymore'."

"You mean Igor did something magical?"

"That's one way to put it," I said. "The other way to put it is that Igor did something to the package that we didn't spot. The other HVAC implants OK?"

"They put them all to sleep except this one," said Menno.

That didn't leave me with a particularly warm, fuzzy feeling, so I got on the opscom to my contact at the Fort.

---

[24] Translator's note: A powershell is a task-based command-line shell and scripting language used to control computers remotely.

"What's the word on the Bears' HVAC implant at State?"

"It's weird. They found a crypto-coin miner running on the port you specified, but it was sending the coins that it mined to the North Koreans," typed my contact.

A bright light went on in the cavernous darkness of my brain, and I could see what the Wizard of Oz, aka Igor, was doing behind the curtain.

"Just what I needed to know," I typed. "It's a wonderful thing. Don't believe any of that hogwash about the North Koreans. I'll get back to you."

I went over to Saskia's terminal, and waited quietly until she acknowledged my presence.

"Sas, I want you to take a look at the code for the HVAC package that the Bears deployed and tell me what happens after the crypto-coin miner in it is discovered by the defenders and purged."

"A stay-behind package concealed in a hijacked scheduled task wakes up in three months and calls home. That was in the report that I sent to Herr[25] van Nispen tot Pannerden," said Saskia imitating a Hitler mustache on her upper lip with two fingers. "Didn't he let you see it?"

I couldn't decide which was the more pressing problem: the stay-behind HVAC package or the iceberg between

---

[25] Translator's note: The German word *Herr* means *Mister*. In this context, the use of this German honorific with reference to a Dutch person is a concealed allusion to WWII and the German occupation of Holland. In other words, it is a big insult.

Saskia and Floris. If Saskia was right—I had little reason to doubt that—I had three months to deal with the stay-behind package, while the problem of Saskia and Floris was more urgent.

That night I asked Kathy if she knew Trien van Nispen tot Pannerden.

"Trieneke, as in Floris' mother?!" said Kathy. "I had lunch with her and Caroline just last week. What's my knowing Trieneke got to do with anything?"

"Well, there's this little problem about Floris' pregnant girlfriend Saskia. Floris thinks his parents would never approve."

"Trieneke not approve of a Kortekaas?! Why I think she dated one of them. I can't remember which, either the father or the uncle. And big Floris, ha! She'd remind him that when they met, she was selling potatoes at a stall on the open-air market on Stevinstraat in Scheveningen on Thursdays."

"Could you arrange a lunch with Trieneke somewhere near the office so you two could casually bump into Saskia, for a 'chance' meeting between the two of them?"

"If I tell her what the real reason for the lunch is, it shouldn't be a problem. What's a good day?"

"The office was planning pizza take-out for lunch on Wednesday. How about that? I could co-opt Saskia to come help me carry the stuff. We always send two people when we get pizza."

"And we'll have a table inside where you can see us on your way to the take-out counter, that the idea?"

"Exactly."

And so a cunning plan took shape. It had to be a secret from both Floris and Saskia, but I had to enlist Menno, who was actually the person I was scheduled to go with for pizza that Wednesday. He'd been in on the problem of Floris, Saskia, and the baby from the start. I was prepared to make him an offer he couldn't refuse, but he agreed without extra inducement. All I needed from him was a plausible reason for him not to be able to go to the pizzeria.

"If you're incapacitated," I said, "I can co-opt Saskia to help me do the lunch run."

On Wednesday, Menno came in with a cane and his left foot in a medical walking boot. Trust Menno to get some great props to go with his story. He always does things up right.

Come lunch time, I headed over to Saskia, and said, "Sas, why don't you come with me to the pizzeria today? Menno is *hors de combat*, and the exercise will do you good."

"I wish everybody would quit looking out for me. I'm only pregnant. I'm not sick or injured."

"In that case, Miss Joan of Arc, Defender of the Feminist Way of Life, Menno is incapacitated, so get up and get your jacket, and come help me carry the pizza back."

"Since you put it that way, kind sir," she said as she got up, leaning a little more on her desk for support than I thought normal, or maybe that was my imagination.

As we walked into the pizzeria, Kathy and Trieneke were strategically seated at a table for four. Kathy waved, and motioned us over to their table.

"Come on, Saskia," I said. "I can't ignore Kathy. We'll just drop by and say 'Hello! We can't stay for long. The pizza should be ready any second now."

It was warm inside the pizzeria, and Saskia unbuttoned her coat, which made the text on her T-shirt plainly visible.

Compiling, please wait

Estimated time remaining: 6 months

"Hi, schat[26]," I said to Kathy. "We're the duty go-fers, going fer pizza to bring back to the office."

"Any who's this lovely young woman with you? You didn't tell me you had lovely young women in the office."

"Didn't I mention Saskia?" I said as guilelessly as I could manage. "She's Floris' girlfriend."

Saskia glared at me.

"Floris' girlfriend!" gushed Kathy with a bit more surprise than I thought was warranted. "Then you must sit down for a minute, my dear! This is Floris' mother."

---

[26] Translator's note: *schat* is a Dutch term of endearment, like *darling*.

The trap sprung silently, but forcefully shut.

"But we have to pick up the pizza and take it back to the office," I protested on cue.

"Just run along to the take-out counter and pay for your pizza. That'll give us a chance to get acquainted with Saskia. She can come help you when you're ready."

That was my cue to exit stage left.

"Coffee for our new guest," said Trieneke to the waiter, who was clearly in on the plot, as he had a cup of coffee and cookie on the table before Saksia could say anything.

The pizza wasn't ready when I got to the counter. Kathy later told me that she had added a little extra icing to our already cunning plan.

She explained that she slipped the manger €20, and told him: "A Mr. Holbrook will call with an order for a large number of pizzas. When he does, please just wait 5 minutes before starting his order. I want to have some extra time to talk with his companion when they come in to collect the pizzas."

When all my pizzas were eventually ready, I signaled to Saskia to come help me. It was a big stack of pizza boxes. The interrogation team let Saskia go, and she came over to help me carry the boxes back to the office. It really was too much for one person to carry.

"That was a set-up," she said, once we were outside again.

"Set-up?"

"Don't play innocent with me. You and Kathy set me up to meet Floris' mother."

"If you say so," I replied as innocently as possible.

"Now I'm invited to join Floris when he comes to have dinner with his parents tonight. 'Tell him he can't come, if he doesn't bring you,' says his mother," moaned Saskia.

"That sounds pleasant enough."

"And she dated my uncle, for Christ's sake!" said Saskia. "Floris will have a cow when I tell him. He bought his new car from my uncle."

"I got my car from your uncle, too."

"We're not dressing for dinner," she says. "Come as you are!" she says. I'll show her! I do have a dress. ... I wonder if I can still get in it."

I tried to imagine Saskia in a dress, but couldn't get the image to focus.

When we got back to the office with the pizza, Saskia and Floris had a long conversation that didn't include any food. At least she didn't deck him again — that afternoon.

The next morning, neither of the combatants said anything to each other. That didn't bode well for the results of the dinner the night before.

Floris went out at lunch and came back with a 'present' for Saskia. It was a T-shirt, black of course, with white letters. It said:

HTTP 418

To a non-hacker 'HTTP 418' just looks like a random collection of characters, you know, the result of letting a monkey play with a typewriter — nothing to get excited about. To Saskia it was a reason to slug Floris again, harder.

"She's not going to make a habit of this I hope," said the nurse in the med center when Menno and I wheeled Floris in. ... He'll need stitches ..."

149

"And you want to hold him to see if he has a concussion," I said finishing the nurse's sentence.

"The naughty desk hit us again?" asked the nurse.

"Yes," said Floris, holding a paper towel to his bleeding forehead.

At least he was still trying to be gallant, despite having insulted Saskia with the T-shirt.

"Why'd she slug him?" asked Menno as we took the chair back to the office.

"Because the HTTP code on the shirt is a huge insult to someone in Saskia's condition."

"It's not one I recognize," said Menno.

"It was the 1998 April Fool's Day joke from our friends at the Internet Engineering Task Force, the people who define HTTP protocols. It's an error status message, like HTTP 404 means 'page not found'. HTTP 418 is from the 'Hyper Text Coffee Pot Control Protocol standard'. It's the error message that should be returned when a command is sent to a teapot telling it to make coffee. The official gloss for HTTP 418 is: 'Any command to brew coffee sent to a teapot should result in the error code 418 (I'm a teapot)'."

"That's all well and good," said Menno, "but what's the insult?"

"I was getting to that. The rest of the gloss says: 'The reporting entity will invariably be short and stout.' It's a veiled quote from a children's nursery rhyme ..."

"Oh, yeah," said Menno, "'I'm a little teapot, short and stout. Here is my handle and here is my spout'."

"That's the one."

"So this T-shirt really says 'I'm short and stout?'" asked Menno.

"You got it."

"No wonder she hit him, "said Menno. "Any expectant father with good sense should know better than to tell the woman pregnant with his child that she's fat. Didn't his father teach him anything about women? "

"Apparently not. That must have been a real fun evening they had at his parents' house last night. … His mother invited Saskia to come to dinner and told her to bring Floris."

"The house still standing?"

"I don't know. I'll have to ask Kathy. She knows Floris' mother, and will have all the dope."

"Trieneke says that the atmosphere was a little strained last night, but nobody threw anything and nobody hit anybody."

"Did Saskia have on a dress?" I asked.

"Yes, as a matter of fact," replied Kathy.

I still couldn't picture it.

Whack a Hack

Cozy Bear's State Department implant woke up as scheduled on February 2nd, Ground Hog Day. Punxsutawney Phil didn't see his shadow, and we didn't see the shadow of the take from State until the 4th, time enough for the stay-behind to go back into hibernation before the defenders could be made aware that it was active and take action against it.

"That's a pretty cool idea," said Menno, "delaying the delivery of the collection from the implant so that we can't report on its activity in real time."

"You think they suspect that we're watching?" asked Floris.

"It's a possibility," I replied. "We did close down their previous hack into State in a day."

I whipped out a situation report:

IMMEDIATE
T O P S E C R E T SAVOY
LIM/DIS NOFORN
SUBJ: Cozy Bear Phishing Attack Against HVAC Control System at US Department of State Resumes Activity
04FE16 14:47Z

The Cozy Bear stay-behind inserted in the HVAC control system for The Department of State on 02 November 2015 resumed activity on 02 February, exactly as predicted by an analysis of the implant's code.

Using its foothold in the HVAC system, the implant gained access to The State Department eMail system and exfiltrated twenty-four hours' worth of eMails from 08:37 01 February to 08:37 Washington local. The highest classification seen was TOP SECRET.

Collector was unable to report the activity of the implant in real-time, because Cozy Bear delayed retrieval of the implant's collection via a password-protected 'dead drop' on the cloud until 04 February. This delay greatly increases the security of Cozy Bear's operation by denying the collector knowledge of the implant's activity when it is most vulnerable to counter-actions by the victim computer's defenders.

Twenty-four hours' worth is a lot of eMails, and the Bears spent the next three days issuing reports from the take. One that was getting a lot of open source media coverage was:

СОВЕРШЕННО СЕКРЕТНО СОРОКА

Former SecState (a named US person) had TOP SECRET material on her Personal eMail Server

The continuing review of the eMails from the personal account of Former SecState (a named US person) determined that they did contain TOP SECRET information. A decision has been made at the highest level of The State Department to withhold the publication of twenty-two of her eMails for this reason.

The unredacted TOP SECRET eMails referenced in the report above were analyzed and reported individually in a more restricted reporting series marked with the covername БАЖАНТ (BAZhANT, PHEASANT).

СОВЕРШЕННО СЕКРЕТНО БАЖАНТ

TOP SECRET eMail Sent by Former SecState (a named US person) #1

Even if it is being reported in the open media, you still want to report it to prove to the consumer that the media got the story right. They don't always, and that's when you can shine by showing the difference between what the media said and what the people on the inside were saying.

One by one, exactly three months from the date that their crypto-coin miners were discovered and neutralized, the HVAC stay-behinds at The White House, The House Office Buildings, The Senate Office Buildings, The Pentagon, and The FBI Office Building woke up from hibernation, collected a day's worth of eMail, exfiltrated it to a password-protected dead drop on the cloud, and went back to sleep.

Twenty-four hour's worth of eMails from The White House covered a lot of territory, but, strangely, the first report out the door from the Bears was the one on PotUS and his concerns about wi-fi coverage in The White House.

СОВЕРШЕННО СЕКРЕТНО СОРОКА

PotUS and Family Lament Spotty Wi-Fi Coverage in The White House

PotUS complained to his IT team that he was dissatisfied with the wi-fi coverage in The White House. "There are lots of dead spots," lamented PotUS, adding that "my wife and daughters are past irritated by the problems with it." PotUS asked, somewhat tongue in cheek, if the work might be completed before the next occupant moves in.

"Why do you think they're so interested in the wi-fi in The White House?" asked Floris.

"Maybe they are working on a way to infect one of the wi-fi nodes, or even the whole network of them, from their new perch, and they need to generate some support for an increase in their budget," I replied.

"I hadn't thought of that. It would be a great coup, if they could pull it off," said Floris. "Maybe if I suggested that something like that was in the offing, I could get more money for next year's budget as well."

"Why don't you give that a try?" I replied.

The Monday after Valentine's Day (Sunday) was marked in the office by an outbreak of T-shirts with more or less romantic hacker rhymes. Sjoerd advertised his availability for hacker girls with a T-shirt that read:

Roses are #FF000[27]
Violets are #000FF
If you can read this,
Then don't be al000FF

Menno advertised his non-availability for hacker girls with a T-shirt that proclaimed:

Roses are #FF000
Violets are #000FF
I Love Sylvia.
This T-shirt's no sp000FF

Saskia belabored the obvious with a T-shirt that said:

Roses are #FF000
Violets are #000FF
I'm having a baby
Here is the pr000FF

I had on an old T-shirt that Kathy had bought me years ago for Valentine's Day.

L0v3 1s l1ke h4ck1ng
0nly a l337 f3w
kn0w h0w t0 d0 IT
I c4n d0 b07h

What was, perhaps, most significant about Valentine's Day +1 at the office was that Floris brought roses for Saskia

---

[27] Translator's note: For those who are not HTML literate, #FF000 is the hexadecimal color code for web-safe red, and #000FF is the code for blue.

and she didn't belt him one. I overheard Saskia explain why to Sjoerd while I was at the coffee pot getting a fresh cup.

"With my new center of gravity," explained Saskia, "I'm more likely to fall down than to land a good one on him, and it's hard to get back up again."

"Yeah, I hear you talking," said Sjoerd, curling a five-kilo barbell in his left hand. "You have to have a stable base to land a good punch."

The FBI HVAC implant woke up on the 25th. The take generated a stack of reports. The Presidential elections in the States were obviously high on the Bears' reporting requirements list. One of the first reports they sent out was:

СОВЕРШЕННО СЕКРЕТНО СОРОКА
FBI Agents Discuss the Possible Blowback from the Investigation into the Use of (a named US person)'s Personal eMail Server for Government Business

A senior FBI Lawyer commented to an FBI Counterintelligence Agent assigned to the investigation of (a named US person)'s use of her personal email server for government business that there was a potential for blowback for the FBI if (a named US person) became President, because the number of agents and prosecutors assigned to the case suggested that the investigation was very aggressive. "She might be our next President," said the Lawyer. "The last thing you need is us going in there loaded for bear. You think she's going to remember or care that it was more DOJ than FBI?"

We hit a lull in the flow of reports coming out of Cozy Bear from their HVAC penetrations in the last week of February. That looked like a good time to ask the three people who knew as much, if not more than the Bears, about the code in the Bears' HVAC stay-behind packages.

"Sas," I said, "you told me when all this began that the stay-behind package would call home in three months, right?"

"That's right. It called home right on time, didn't it?"

"Did it?" I replied. "Why didn't someone tell me that it had called home?"

"It was in the logs," said Menno, typing furiously in search of a copy of the log for the call home from the first stay-behind.

The screen in front of him painted and Menno pointed at a line with a time hack, an IP address, and an 8-bit character: 0100 0100, which in people speak is the ASCII letter 'D'.

"Was I supposed to recognize that as 'ET calls home'?"

"I did," said Saskia. "I figured you would, too."

"No, I didn't. Can we assume for a minute that I'm really dense?"

"Assume!?" said Sjoerd.

I knew better than to react to Sjoerd's comment, and continued: "And have you explain all the steps involved in a 'call home'. ... Well, don't everybody answer at once. Menno?"

"The stay-behind sends an 8-bit character to a reflection server mimicking the behavior of legitimate users. The reflection server passes the character to the Bears. The Bears' computer responds with a shortened URL that directs the stay-behind to a server with an image carrying a steganographic payload that tells the stay-behind what to do, and where to send the result. If anybody at the victim computer notices the image download, it's just an ordinary image to the naked eye."

"Is there anything we can target?" I asked.

"The reflection server and the image server are wiped the minute they complete their task, and are never used again," said Saskia.

"And we're not even sure where the stay-behind is located," said Sjoerd. "It could be on the HVAC machine, or on the main host; on a normally unused part of the hard drive; or on a router or wi-fi box."

"All the text stings in the modules are encrypted to defeat string searches for known malware," added Menno, "and the package shuts down if it detects forensic tools in use."

"So even if we alerted the defenders to the 'call home,' …"

"We don't know who called home. It could be any of the stay-behinds. They all sent the same character in the call home," replied Saskia.

"And we don't know when the stay-behind will be told to start work. It could be today, tomorrow, the day after, or next week," continued Menno.

"I get the picture. If the defenders don't see it active when we send an alert that it called home, they'll think we're just crying 'Wolf!' and go away."

"It's a great piece of social engineering," said Menno. "They talked about things like this at Black Hat."

"So we're stuck with only being able to report after the fact," I said. "Better than nothing, but reporting in real time is where budget, promotions and cash awards come from."

Cozy Bear reporting from The Pentagon eMail cache had a bunch of very interesting items, but the one that was closest to my — and the Cozy Bears' — hearts was the one on the line item budget increase for cybersecurity in fiscal year 2017.

СОВЕРШЕННО СЕКРЕТНО СОРОКА

Pentagon Requests Almost US$1 Billion Increase in FY2017 Budget for Cybersecurity

The budget proposal put forth by The Pentagon for FY2017 includes US$6.7 billion for cyber operations, an increase of US$0.9 billion compared to the budget that was enacted for FY2016. The justification that went forward with the budget proposal said the additional funds are necessary for "new cyber strategies that focus on building cyber capabilities and organizations for The Department of Defense's three primary cyber missions: 1) to defend DoD networks, systems, and information; 2) to defend the Nation against cyberattacks of significant consequence; and 3) to provide cyber support to operational and contingency plans."

"I wonder if there will be any spillover from this for us?" asked Floris.

"I'd make sure the Director's Daily Brief included this one," I replied.

Cross Bears

"Hey, Floris," said Menno, who had 'The Watch', take a look at Bear Chat. Igor is complaining to Sasha that the охуённые вояки (expletive military types) have broken into the DNC computer and are thrashing around like a drunken bull in a china shop. The a**holes are making such a mess that even the three blind mice who run security for the DNC will notice."

Sasha's response was a Russian expletive that I'd never seen written down before. The last time I'd heard it was … no, wait, this is one of those 'if I told you, I'd have to shoot you stories,' so let's just forget it.

Sasha got up and walked over to Igor's terminal, and they spent about five minutes gesticulating and pounding on the desk, destroying Igor's keyboard in the process. Sasha walked back to his terminal, and called up a message blank.

TO: Moscow Center, ATTN: GRU Liaison

GRU Spec Cyber Ops was noted this date in a heavy-handed penetration of target US90573 which we have been successfully exploiting since August 2015. The penetration is so clumsy that even the inept cyber defenders will undoubtedly notice it in short order if it is not withdrawn, prompting defensive measures against the GRU penetration that will endanger our operation, for which Moscow Center has repeatedly expressed its great appreciation.

I thought that was a very reserved message, considering the expletive he'd used when Igor told him about it.

The next two hours, it was one (expletive) post after another from Igor on Bear Chat, describing what kind of carnage the 'military guys' were wreaking on the DNC server, and how horrible his new keyboard was.

Just after lunch (our local), Sasha got a chat from a buddy named Vasilij at Moscow Center. It said:

Sasha, don't send that 'Query Status' I know you're itching to send. Your GRU message blew up like a bomb here, and it's gonna be discussed at the very top, with P. So keep your head down, and rein in that temper of yours, otherwise the men in black may come knocking at your door. Cheers, Vasilij

"I'm taking the rest of the day off," wrote Sasha on Bear Chat. "Igor's in charge. No messages to the outside world while I'm gone, and if anyone asks for me, tell 'em I'm in the toilet."

He didn't sound like he was in a good mood.

After that, Igor quit complaining about the GRU penetration of the DNC computer. None of the Russians, in fact, said much of anything for the rest of the afternoon.

Long about 16:30 Local Menno strolled over to Floris' position.

"Floris, you remember what happened last year on April 15th?" asked Menno.

"No, but I'm sure you do," replied Floris.

"April 15th is День специалиста по радиоэлектронной борьбе Вооруженных сил России (Day of the Russian Armed Forces Radio-Electronic Warfare Specialist), and last year Cozy Bear didn't even open up shop on that day. It was a Wednesday, and we were taken by surprise."

"And your point is?" asked Floris.

"A three-day weekend," said Menno. "The 15th is on Friday."

Floris' eyes lit up, and his smile broadened a bit.

"A liberal leave policy will be in effect for Friday the 15th. It is a Russian holiday and the target is not expected in to work," said the chat message that Floris sent.

I don't know what had made Floris smile at the thought of a day off, but whatever Floris was planning for the 15th, the 15th had other plans for Floris. Saskia went into labor two weeks early at 04:23 Local. Kathy and I were sensibly asleep at that time, so the story that follows is third hand.

Saskia was already on maternity leave, and staying with her parents. Saskia waited to wake them up until the contractions were five minutes apart, which was cutting it too close as far as her father was concerned. He got behind the wheel of his car and put the pedal to the metal.

Seven minutes and thirty-nine seconds from their door to the ER with a cop car in pursuit. The sight of an obviously pregnant lady being hurriedly wheeled off to the maternity ward convinced the cops not to give Kees a ticket.

Saskia's mother barely had enough time to call Floris' mother from the car on the way to the hospital as arranged.

Trieneke called 'little' Floris and told him that if he wasn't at the hospital before she got there that she'd never let him forget it. Then she woke up 'big' Floris and told him to drive slowly so their son could beat them to the hospital.

'Little' Floris got to the hospital — speeding ticket in hand — six minutes before his mother. He'd have been twelve minutes ahead of her if it hadn't been for the cops. It's hard to convince the cops that you're on your way to deliver a baby with no pregnant lady in the car and no obstetrician's license.

By the time the two mothers press-ganged 'little' Floris into some surgical scrubs, and through the door of the delivery room, the contractions were under two minutes apart.

On his arrival at her side, Saskia is reported to have said something like: "Damn you! This hurts! Give me a kiss and hold my hand!" That sounds mighty restrained for Saskia, but this is, after all, a fourth-hand report.

When I got into work on Monday the 18th, Floris was handing out *beschuit met muisjes*, a typically Dutch tradition to celebrate the arrival of a baby. Literally, the name of this treat means *rusks with mice*. Dutch rusks are twice-baked, crunchy round toasts about a half inch thick and three inches in diameter. The mice are really sugar-coated aniseeds with their tails sticking out. Butter is smeared on the rusks to give the mice something to hold on to. The mice are blue for a boy and pink for a girl. When the King and Queen celebrated their daughters' births, the company that makes *muisjes* did a special run in orange, the national color of the Netherlands and of the royal family.

Floris' mice were blue.

I'm not really fond of the taste of aniseed, but you can't refuse.

"Take two," said Floris. "It's twins!"

"Congratulations!" I said, shaking his hand as a prelude to taking two.

"Let me show you the pictures," said Floris, pulling out his cell phone. Normally, he knew better than to bring his phone into the enclosure, but his excitement about the twins got the better of him. Having twins is a semi-reasonable excuse for forgetting to check your cell phone at the door. If he did it again, though, we'd have to write him up.

Menno, Sjoerd, and I quickly ushered him out of the shielded enclosure so he could show us the pictures.

This also got me out of having to eat the aniseed. By the time Floris got back in the shielded enclosure—less his cell phone—it was too late for him to figure out who had and who hadn't.

Floris' enthusiasm for the twins made it obvious to everyone that—contrary to numerous, heated recriminations about 'the baby' between Floris and: Saskia, the grandmothers, and the grandfathers—the twins had him wrapped around their little fingers.

"Want to get in the pool about when the wedding will be?" asked Menno. "There's a three-week minimum wait time to book the civil ceremony."

"I'll take the first available Monday for the civil ceremony," I said, figuring that they hadn't had time to go get a license on Friday.

"That's the 9th," said Menno.

I lost. So did everybody else. It was Friday the 6th for the civil ceremony and Saturday for the Church. We were all invited.

The bride actually wore a dress, white with a long train.

"I've never seen Saskia in a dress," said Sjoerd. "And I'm not a hundred-percent sure, but I don't think I've ever seen her in something white."

The groom had on an obviously expensive suit.

"The suit must be off the rack," said Menno. "He didn't have time to get one custom made."

"It's an old suit of his father's," said Kathy, who'd been a part of the planning committee.

"And the dress?" asked Menno.

"It's Trieneke's," replied Kathy

"That's pretty weird," said Menno. "Wearing your mother-in-law's wedding gown."

"Femke wanted her daughter's gown to be better than hers was," replied Kathy. "Hers was the same dress she wore to church every week. And besides, she doesn't have it anymore. Trieneke's dress fits Saskia exactly. She didn't have to have it altered, unlike the suit."

"This is a pretty good spread," said Menno with a glass of champagne in his hand as Kathy and I walked into the reception tent. "Look, they've got crab salad and pâté."

"That's not all there is," said Kathy, pulling on my arm to take me towards another table in the far corner that had *bitterballs* and *saucijzenbroodjes*[28]. We left 'big' Floris and Menno at the 'classy' food table where they were discussing Wittgenstein, and went over to join Sjoerd and Simon at the 'cheap eats' table, where they were discussing which beer to try — I counted six different kinds.

"Yeah, the champagne's OK," said Simon, "but I prefer beer with my *bitterballs*."

"I couldn't agree more," said Kathy.

After their session with the photographer, the bride and groom changed into their normal clothes for the reception. Saskia had on a black T-shirt that said:

K339 c4lm, 7w1ns
M0m's a h4ck3r

Floris' T-shirt said:

L337 f47h3r 0f 7w1ns

Floris was pushing the stroller with the twins in it. They were asleep, much to the annoyance of their grandmothers.

"Big Floris wanted a live band," said Kathy, "but Trieneke said that a live band would be too loud for the twins, and Saskia insisted that the twins be at the reception."

The recorded music was played on an underpowered sound system that ensured that it would not be too loud for

---

[28] Translator's note: *Bitterballs* are crispy bite-size, deep-fried breadcrumb-covered balls of minced beef or veal. *Saucijzenbroodjes* are like American 'pigs in a blanket,' except that the 'pigs' are sausages instead of hot dogs. These are typical Dutch snack bar foods.

the twins. You couldn't even tell there was music at the 'cheap eats' table. It was too far away.

Saskia and Floris pretended to dance. Neither one of them knew how. After that came the traditional dances with the father of the bride, the father of the groom and the best man (Menno). Saskia then sat down and refused to get up from her chair to dance with anyone else.

"Can you blame her?" asked Kathy. "I'll bet the twins haven't been letting her get much sleep."

Saskia sent Floris over to get her some *bitterballs*. I couldn't blame here about that either. They were good.

Floris was in at work on Monday.

"Honeymoon?" said Floris. "Who's got time for a honeymoon when you've got twins?"

He looked a little tired himself. I took that as a good sign that he was splitting the night shifts taking care of the twins with Saskia.

Little did we know at the time, but Floris and Saskia's wedding took place on the same day that the DNC—after ignoring the FBI warnings about Cozy Bear for nine months—finally hired an IT Security Consultant to clean up their system. The consultant quickly found and confirmed the penetration of the DNC computer network by the GRU hackers, covernamed Fancy Bear. It would, however, be more than a month before we learned about it from *The New York Times*.

Summer in the Bear Lair

May

It was Monday, the 9th of May, and things were slow, because the Bears had the day off for Victory Day, the official Russian celebration of the end of WWII. Menno brought me a report that had gone out from the Bears on the 6th. We were only just getting to see it, because 5, 6, 7, and 8 May was a long weekend for us. The 5th was the Dutch holiday to celebrate Liberation Day, as in the day that the Germans officially surrendered in Holland at the end of WWII. It was an official holiday, so the office was closed. Since the 5th was a Thursday, and the wedding was on Friday the 6th, the whole office took an extra day of leave, which made it a four-day weekend. That put us a little behind in reading through the take.

When things slowed down from the "now you see 'em, now you don't" HVAC penetrations, the Bears would dip into the DNC eMails and report stuff. This was poaching on somebody's turf, because, normally, all the DNC collection was automatically forwarded to the Центр (Center) analysts across town working the project. Anything that the Bears reported from the DNC was, therefore, interesting enough to grab one of the Bears' attention before it went across town. This one in particular also caught Menno's attention.

The report read:

СОВЕРШЕННО СЕКРЕТНО СОРОКА

US Democratic Party Officials Discuss Targeting a Democratic Candidate for President for his Religious Views

(named US person A), an official of the Democratic National Committee, suggested that an effort be made to discredit (named US person B), a candidate for the Democratic Party nomination for President, by demonstrating that he is an atheist, instead of a Jew. (named US person A) stated that "My Southern Baptist peeps would draw a big difference between a Jew and an atheist."

Menno stormed over to my terminal with a print of the report. He was indignant.

"I just can't believe it," he said, plopping the printout down in the middle of my keyboard, which made it hard to keep typing. "They're going to attack (a named US Presidential Candidate) for being an atheist?!"

I think Menno's objection was a result of the (in)famous Dutch tolerance of all religious beliefs. The Dutch were proud of having offered refuge to the Jews during the Inquisition in Spain, and of the legacy of Anne Frank — the lines to get in the museum always run around the block. These days, though the King of the House of Orange is Protestant, the Queen is a Catholic, and the latest polls show that atheists outnumber theists 25% to 17%. The majority of the population is either agnostic (about 31%) or spiritual without belonging to an organized religion (27%). I'd never even considered asking Menno what his religious beliefs were. He'd either have been insulted that I felt compelled to ask such a stupid question, or have answered Discordianist, Neo-pagan, or Zen Buddhist just to under-score the irrelevance of this question with regard to him.

"What relevance do his religious beliefs have to his ability to govern the country?"

"Depends on whom you ask. America's a free country, and everybody's entitled to their own opinion, no matter how ill-informed."

"You mean the logic of this report is correct?"

"Oh, absolutely."

"I didn't meet anyone at MIT, at Black Hat or DEF CON to whom it would have made any difference."

"But they probably weren't from Kentucky or West Virginia," I replied.

"How can you live in such a benighted country?"

"It has certain other advantages that compensate for that."

"And now I suppose you're going to tell me that you don't have a requirement to report this kind of information?"

"Yes, and no," I replied, reminding myself of Tolkien's advice about asking a question of the Elves. "On the one hand, I have a requirement to report the fact that the Bears reported on this topic from their take from the DNC server. On the other hand, I have a strict prohibition on reporting the content of the eMails between US persons, as in 'I can go to jail if I do'. So, if you'd brought me the raw eMail, and demanded I report it, I would have declined as politely as I could; but since you brought me a report from the Bears, I can report that."

"Well, what are you waiting for?"

"I can take a hint," I said. I removed the print-out from my keyboard and my fingers started dancing out a report.

June

"Who's the target for June, Sasha?" said Boris when he came in on June 1st.

"The Center for a New American Security," replied Sasha. "A hot-shot Washington D.C. Think Tank."

I dutifully typed up a situation report.

ROUTINE
T O P S E C R E T SAVOY
LIM/DIS NOFORN
SUBJ: Cozy Bear Preparing a Phishing Attack Against a
Washington D.C. Based Think Tank
01JN16 08:23Z
Cozy Bear announced that the phishing target of the
month of June will be the Washington D.C. based Think
Tank 'The Center for a New American Security'.
Analysis of the time lines of previous attacks carried out
this year suggests that the spear-phishing volley will be
launched on 15 June.

After the Bears had gone home on the 10th, the DNC server implant ceased functioning. When the Bears came in on Monday, they tried to revive the implant, but to no avail.

Sasha took the news rather calmly.

"I told them that the (expletive) GRU would (expletive) things up. But would they listen? No!"

He didn't include the 'I told you so' in his report on the loss of access. He just stuck with the facts.

"The DNC implant ceased communications with control at 22:47 Moscow time on 10 June."

We didn't find out what really happened until the 15th.

"Get a load of this," said Sjoerd who was on 'The Watch'. "Boris just pulled up a *New York Times* article on their DNC penetration."

DNC Says Russian Hackers Penetrated Its Files, Including Dossier on (a named US person)
June 14, 2016

WASHINGTON — Two groups of Russian hackers, working for competing government intelligence agencies, penetrated computer systems of the Democratic National Committee and gained access to emails, chats and a trove of opposition research against (a named US person), according to the Party and a cybersecurity firm.

"Get that translated into Russian," said Sasha. "I want to send it to the Center."

From Sasha's perspective, it was a great article, because it showed that he was right: the GRU penetration of the DNC computer was the beginning of the end for Cozy Bear's implant there. He didn't seem sorry to see it end, however. There was much more cursing and gnashing of teeth when the Bears lost State, The White House, and The Pentagon in the Fall of 2104.

I sort of had to agree with Sasha's lack of sorrow for the loss of the target. It wasn't the most interesting entity to collect against; all the material coming from DNC was automatically forwarded to the Center. The Bears would poach the occasional eMail from the DNC if they were bored and it was interesting enough, but those were few and far between.

We were even less involved with the DNC than the Bears. All we had to do was send out a weekly status report that said: "Cozy Bear penetration of the DNC computer system continues active as before." That's not what you'd call an analytic or intellectual challenge. It's not even enough typing to make your fingers tired.

Fortunately, the Bears weren't really that bored. They had the HVAC 'pop-ups' reporting to keep them warm. In between 'pop-ups' they had been carefully establishing perches at an array of Think Tanks and NGOs. That's what Boris' question about the 'target of the month' was all about.

The prep for a phishing attack to establish a perch lasted three days. The first two days were used for research on the target, while the last day was spent crafting the lures and cover eMails. They always launched the attack on the 15th of the month, or the Friday before the 15th, if the 15th came during the weekend. If they got a foothold, which they almost always did, they would establish persistence, and evaluate the materials they could access, before putting their implant to sleep to be awakened when needed at a later date.

If it wasn't for the loss of the DNC implant and *The New York Times* article, it would have been an anticlimax to write the follow-up that said our analysis of the launch date of the phishing volley was correct. After five targets of the month, the time line had become routine.

There's nothing like the loss of a target to ruin a collector's day, however. I was afraid that the launch of the phishing volley against the target for June would be postponed.

I needn't have worried. Sasha's team had things firmly in hand.

"The show must go on," said Igor. "Пуск! (Pusk!, Launch!)"

ROUTINE
T O P   S E C R E T SAVOY
LIM/DIS NOFORN
SUBJ: Cozy Bear Launched a Phishing Attack Against a Washington D.C. Based Think Tank
15JN16 16:11Z
Cozy Bear launched a volley of 127 phishing eMails against The Center for a New American Security, a Washington D.C. based Think Tank. The attack appears to be a success, as there have thus far been three phish who have bitten on the malicious packages in the lures eMailed to them.

When the Bears came back on the 16th, Igor said, "I hope there's something more exciting on their server than what we've found on the others."

"Yeah, I know what you mean," said Boris. "I'm tired of downloading stuff that the Embassy has already bought and paid for. That's not going to get us more trips to Black Hat."

"Yeah, yeah, yeah," said Sasha. "Get the address harvester running. This is a strategic op. The payoff will come when we use this as a perch to launch an attack that will get us something really juicy."

"Sasha, you see *The Washington Post* for the 15th?" asked Igor.

"Parts of it. Which article?"

"The one about the DNC." The title is 'Russia Denies DNC Hack and Says Maybe Someone «forgot the password»'," said Igor. "According to the Kremlin, we didn't do it."

"ROTFLMAO," typed Sasha. "I loved the part where Klimenko said it's always easier to explain away the stupidity of setting the password to '123456' by saying it was the intrigues of your enemies than to admit your own incompetence."

"I'm insulted. I thought the hack was more subtle than that," said Igor.

July

"Boris, you see *The Washington Post* for the 22nd?" asked Natasha.

"I'll bet you mean the article on the *Wikileaks* dump," said Boris.

"You think it came from the Center?"

"It didn't come from here."

"Must have been the (expletive) military," said Igor.

The State Department 'Whack a Hack' implant resumed activity on the 24th, and the first report out of the chute from the Bears was on the appointment of a new Chief Information Officer for State. I could see how they thought that was a high-priority piece of info.

СОВЕРШЕННО СЕКРЕТНО СОРОКА

(a named US person) Appointed the CIO for US Department of State

(a named US person), a member of the Senior Foreign Service with the rank of Minister-Counselor, has been selected to fill the position of the Chief Information Officer for the US Department of State. The appointee will be responsible for information resources and technology initiatives, including the provision of core information, knowledge management, and technology (IT) services to The Department of State and its 260 overseas Missions. He will be directly responsible for the Information Resource Management (IRM) Bureau's budget of US$569 million, and will oversee State's total IT/knowledge management budget of approximately US$1 billion dollars.

He previously served as Information Management Officer Beijing, and Director of Regional Information Management Center (RIMC) Frankfurt, Principal Deputy CIO D.C., Deputy CIO for Foreign Operations D.C., the Dean of the School of Applied Information Technology (SAIT) at the Foreign Service Institute (FSI), and the Director of Information Resource Management's Messaging Systems Office.

When You Come to a Fork in the Flowchart, Take It

August is when most of Europe goes on vacation, but that wasn't why we were shorthanded in the office. We had three travelers at Black Hat/DEF CON. Nobody in the office had school-age children, so we could spread vacation time around as we needed, which was handy, because we had to keep the office manned as long as the Bears weren't going on vacation. Three of them were at Black Hat/DEF CON, too, which made them shorthanded, but they *were* open for business.

Just so the PC police won't come to get me, Saskia was the only woman in the office, and she was on maternity leave, so we were literally keeping the office *manned* in August, that is, until I got an opscom from my contact at the Fort on the 3rd.

"We're starting to get some grumbling from on high about you not being able to report on Cozy Bear in real time so we can shut down the HVAC pop-up hacks," typed my contact.

"The Dutch say that you've gotta row with the oars you've got," I replied.

"Is that an official position from the Host?" asked my contact.

"No, it's just a Dutch proverb."

"In that case, we'd like you to push the matter with the Host a bit harder and see if you can come up with something," was the reply. "If more people, or money, or computer time will help, there seems to be a readiness to supply those."

"OK. I get the picture. I'll talk with the Host and see what we can come up with. Give me till next Monday to get back to you."

"I'm writing it on my calendar in pen," typed my contact.

If he was writing it in pen, that was really, really, seriously the deadline, and we'd have to come up with something. Otherwise, we'd be up to our ears in TDY-ers, who'd be worse than the proverbial too many cooks who spoiled the broth.

Floris, Sjoerd, and Jan were in Las Vegas, so Menno had the con.

"Menno," I explained, "we've got to pull out all the stops and find a solution before they unleash the hordes on us; who will be as likely to break our access to the Bears, as to find a solution to reporting in real time."

"You're the one with all the cunning plans. Cunning away!"

"I want to bring Saskia back to work."

"She's taking care of the twins. She can't come in."

"Oh, sure she can," I replied. "You can bring kids into a secure workspace as long as they can't talk. Check with your security office if you don't believe me."

He checked with security, and Saskia came in after lunch with her double-wide stroller, and enough supplies to have seen Napoleon safely through the winter in Russia.

I explained the problem to Saskia, then she and Menno started taking the code in the stay-behind package apart in every character encoding they could think of.

Simon, Maarten, and I kept the coffee pot going, and the twins entertained, diapered, and fed.

We sent out for pizza. We called Trieneke in to bring more diapers and bottles of milk. Simon went out to get more coffee. I had Kathy bring me in a clean shirt to replace the one that one of the twins had thrown up on.

It was pushing 21:37 Local. The twins were asleep. There was only one slice of pizza left: salami, and it looked far from fresh. There was, however, fresh coffee, and cookies courtesy of Kathy.

"We've tried everything else," said Saskia. "Let's try Unicode."

The screen repainted in Unicode.

"Look at that," said Menno, pointing to the screen. "That looks like the morse code in the Easter Egg signature blocks."

```
[U+200B][U+200B][U+2003][U+200B][U+2003]
[U+2003][U+2003][U+200B][U+2003][U+200B]
[U+2003][U+200B][U+2003]
```

"It spells F-O-R-K."

"Fork!?" said Saskia. "That's a marker for the encryption program. Natasha's notes for the package said that the word 'fork' tells the encryption program where the breaks between the segments are. But I've never been able to find it before."

"If it's a marker," said Menno, "then it won't be encrypted. We can search for this Unicode string to find the package."

"Don't just stand there," I said. "Tell the package to encrypt itself, so we can see if your idea works."

It did, but the search string had to be entered in binary. If you think that's not hard, you should try it sometime. Your eyes will cross and you'll begin to doubt your sanity. The morse for the letter 'F' in Unicode, for example, is

[U+200B][U+200B][U+2003],

but in binary those three Unicode characters look like: 1110001010000000010001011111000101000000100 0101111100010100000001000011.

The next afternoon, I called my contact at the Fort on the opscom.

"You were talking about TDY support?"

"Sure, we can have a team of four out there day after tomorrow."

"Can I have the money you would have spent on that TDY, if we've found the solution?"

He didn't say anything for a while.

"If we can solve a little problem like this, surely you can solve a trifling problem of money for TDY and cash awards."

"It's not a trivial problem," he replied.

"For other people, maybe, but for you, a piece of cake."

"You have a solution?"

"Yes, and part of it calls for having a team from here go to visit the victim computers to apply the patch."

"We can have that done locally."

"No, the host wants it VERY closely held," I typed, "and like you said, applying the patch is a non-trivial problem."

"A team?"

"Two people."

"A cash award?"

"€5,000 each for the two people. They're the ones who found the solution."

"Hm, that might fly if the patch works."

"Don't give me any 'IF'. I'm on-site, and I say the patch works. That's one of the reasons you sent me here."

"What do you need?" he typed. I could almost see him frowning as he typed.

"I need a funding cite for the TDY: business-class air, rent-a-car, ten days per diem, and a handler to get them in at the repair sites."

"And they can fix it?"

"Didn't I say so?"

"When can your team launch?" asked my contact.

"We've got travelers at Black Hat/DEF CON, so we can't launch until the 8th at the earliest; after they get back."

We had the funding cite message for the TDY in less than an hour.

Saskia and Menno flew out on Monday the 8th. Saskia and Floris kissed at the airport as he flew in and she flew out.

Floris wasn't thrilled, but the grandmothers were pleased to take turns watching the twins. Sylvia wasn't pleased about Menno going either, what with the new baby and all. Menno put her on the phone with me so I could convince her that he *really* needed to go on the TDY.

"Is he really going to save the world?" she asked me on the phone.

"Of course," I said, "well, at least a large part of America."

Tuesday the 9th was the team's first call: at The White House. That shows you who's important in D.C..

"The snacks were great," said Saskia when they got back. "And the coffee wasn't bad either. We were out in less than three hours. It took longer to find than we thought it would, because the stay-behind was in a router.

"They gave us a tour after we finished," said Menno. "But we didn't get to see the President."

Wednesday the 10th was The Senate. They were clearly following the protocol list order of things.

"Good thing we were out in under an hour," said Menno during the debriefing. "They didn't even offer us coffee. And I was glad of the handler from the Fort. He kept their IT folks from shoulder surfing while we found the stay-behind and fried it. It was in the HVAC controller."

"They were much more snooty than the people at The White House," said Saskia.

186

Thursday the 11ᵗʰ was The House.

"Our reputation preceded us from the Senate," said Saskia. "They all stayed fifteen feet back, and bowed and scraped. They brought us coffee and sandwiches. It took about two hours to find, because the stay-behind was in a wi-fi box."

On the 11ᵗʰ, while Saskia and Menno were at The House, the Bears cleared the dead drop with the take from the stay-behind at The Pentagon that had woken up on the 9ᵗʰ. The first item the Bears reported was about the F-35.

СОВЕРШЕННО СЕКРЕТНО СОРОКА
Pentagon's Director of Testing Believes That the F-35 Will Not Be Delivered on Time

The Pentagon's Director of Testing, (a named US person), has authored a memo in which he states that the next-generation Fighter Program is "on a path toward failing to deliver" the full capabilities of the F-35 on time. The current deadline for the Developer (Lockheed) to deliver is 2018. The current issues with the plane, according to (a named US person), are a growing number of software problems which interfere with target identification, communications between aircraft, and radar signal detection.

Friday the 12ᵗʰ was The Pentagon.

"A case of the squeaky wheel getting the grease, after your report from the Bears' on the F-35," typed my contact at the Fort. "State was supposed to be next."

"Our escort from their IT shop tried to get fresh," said Saskia, "so I decked him. He should have kept his hands to himself."

"I tried to caution him about the inappropriateness of his behavior, and the physical danger of upsetting Saskia," said Menno, "but he wouldn't listen to me any more than Saskia did, when I cautioned her about wearing her

'1f u c4n r34d 7h1s u r34lly n33d t0 g37 l41d'

T-shirt to The Pentagon."

"I scared the sh*t out of them," typed my Contact at the Fort telling me about the incident. "They were bitching and moaning about the guy having lost two teeth, and wanted to press charges against Saskia. I lied that there'd be a diplomatic incident that would get all the US Defense Attachés at the embassy in the sending country PNG-ed[29] if that turkey was still working in The Pentagon at the end of the day. He was on his way to Thule Air Base, Greenland, before Saskia left the building."

That weekend, Saskia and Menno did the Smithsonian on the Mall, separately.

"The Air and Space Museum was awesome," said Menno. "Imagine being able to see the Spirit of St. Louis, the Apollo 11 command module, and the Friendship 7 capsule all in one building."

"I really enjoyed the Museum of American History," said Saskia. "The computer collection is remarkable. It has everything from punch cards to an Apple 1, to a Cray-2, and Deep Blue, the computer that defeated reigning champion Garry Kasparov in a chess match in 1997."

---

[29] Translator's note: The abbreviation PNG expands to *persona non grata* (*unwelcome person*). This is a piece of diplomatic shorthand for 'Pack Now and Get out of town!' Members of diplomatic missions who are PNG-ed generally have 48 hours to leave the receiving country.

Monday the 15th was the FBI.

"The place was full of suits," said Menno, "even the IT guys."

"But they kept their distance alright," said Saskia. "One of them asked if it was true about the Air Force guy. Our handler assured them it was."

"It took four hours to find the stay-behind. It was in the main frame. It was toast in time for lunch. We went to some Mexican place and had tacos. They were good. You can't get them like that here," said Menno.

Tuesday the 16th was State.

"It wasn't foggy at all," said Saskia.

"The coffee was in china cups," said Menno. "And the suits running around there were more expensive than at the FBI, but at least the IT guys and gals had on T-shirts. The one I liked best said:

Life would be much easier if I had the source code."

Trust Menno to find something philosophical at State. I never have.

They flew back on the 17th, but going to Holland from the States you lose a day, and they didn't get in until the 18th. Floris took off to pick up Saskia.

On the 24th, the Bears were getting a little edgy. The stay-behind at The White House had missed a third comsched.

"Run me a systems check, Boris!" said Sasha.

"I just ran you one five minutes ago."

"Why hasn't the implant at The White House called home yet?, damn it!" said Sasha.

"You learning any new Russian curse words, Menno?" I asked.

"Yeah, Sasha seems to have an inexhaustible supply of new ones."

IMMEDIATE
T O P S E C R E T SAVOY
LIM/DIS NOFORN
SUBJ: Cozy Bear Implant at The White House Fails to Call Home
24AU16 16:03Z
Cozy Bear expressed markedly profanity-laden displeasure that the stay-behind implant at The White House had missed three communications schedules with Cozy Bear. A heavy object was thrown, destroying the office coffee pot, a domestic appliance that is in short supply in Moscow, according to one of the team members.

On the 26th, things got progressively worse. The FBI stay-behind didn't call home, and Sasha was even more displeased than on Wednesday.

IMMEDIATE
T O P S E C R E T SAVOY
LIM/DIS NOFORN
SUBJ: Cozy Bear Implants at the FBI and The White House Fail to Call Home
26AU16 16:13Z
Cozy Bear's profanity-laden diatribe about the failure of the FBI implant to call home would have made a sailor blush. That is the second missed call for the FBI implant.

The stay-behind implant at The White House has missed five communications schedules with Cozy Bear, and Cozy Bear believes it to have been discovered and neutralized.

I called my contact at the Fort and asked: "Now about those cash awards?"

"People are debating €5,000 or €7,000 as we speak."

"Tell them they deserve €10,000."

I had the fund cites by the 30th, and the certificates of award came in the pouch the next week. We did the presentation up right: in the auditorium with the Director to hand them over personally, and shake hands. Saskia brought the twins up onstage with her.

"Ladies, please note," said the Director, "that there is a working life after childbirth. And just to prove that point, I'm proud to present Mrs. Van Nispen tot Pannerden-Kortekaas — and her twins — with this check for €7,000 from our American sister agency for her post-partum contributions to a closely held joint project."

"She is, however, not the only recipient of American largesse. Mr. Huizinga has likewise received €7,000 for his work on the same project. This large sum shows how much our sister agency values our work."

Loose Lips Sink Ships

April the 3rd was a 'Manic Monday,' but the fallout from it didn't reach Holland until Tuesday, because of the time difference between Moscow and Washington. I had taken Monday off so that Kathy and I could go to the Keukenhof to see the tulips without all the crowds that you get in the weekend. The end of March had been warm, so the tulips were out and the whole thing was a sea of color.

"How was the Keukenhof?" asked Sjoerd, as I came in.

"We had a really great time," I said. "Everything was in bloom. You and Trixie should get up there."

"Hey, Floris!" said Sjoerd. "How about tomorrow off?"

"Depends on what the Bears do today, but it's been quiet the last couple of weeks, so in principle, OK."

Manic Monday, however, caught up to us about 10:08 Local.

"Sasha," said Igor on Bear Chat. "Take a look at this article in yesterday's *Washington Post*: 'New Details Emerge about 2014 Russian Hack of The State Department: It was «hand to hand combat»'."

"I don't like the looks of that," said Menno, who had 'The Watch.'

"The looks of what?" asked Floris.

"The looks of the title of the article that Igor just sent over Bear Chat," said Menno, whose dancing fingers were calling up a copy of the article as he spoke.

Floris got up and went over to look over Menno's shoulder. I was on my way back from the coffee pot, so I stopped by to look, too.

The article was about the comments that Deputy Director NSA (a named US person) had made at a presentation hosted by The Washington Ideas Roundtable Series and the Aspen Institute Cybersecurity & Technology Program on March 21st. The presentation was entitled "Cyber Threats: Perspectives from the NSA and FBI."

"They're talking about us," said Menno, pointing at the paragraph that said:

> The NSA was alerted to the compromises by a Western intelligence agency. The ally had managed to hack not only the Russians' computers, but also the surveillance cameras inside their workspace, according to the former officials. They monitored the hackers as they maneuvered inside the US systems and as they walked in and out of the workspace, and were able to see faces, the officials said.

"Saskia, call the Director's office and tell them I have to speak with him immediately," said Floris over his shoulder. "Menno, get me a print of the article."

"Coming up," said Menno, who stopped mid-keystroke in his print command. "I just lost both video feeds from the Bears."

"Quick," said Floris, "Shut down the implant. Tell it to erase itself!"

"But it hasn't run the log clean-up routine yet today," objected Menno.

"I don't care. Shut it down, shut it down now!"

And I thought I'd see Menno type fast before, but this broke all his past speed records. Good thing it was Menno on 'The Watch.' He knew all the implant commands by heart. He didn't have to look them up.

"Implant's toast," said Menno.

"Saskia, tell them sooner than immediately. Five minutes ago would be better than now."

"Menno, my print-out," said Floris.

"It should be in the printer tray already," said Menno.

"The Director is on his way down," said Saskia.

"I didn't mean for him to come down here," said Floris. "I was going up there."

"Whatever," said Saskia. "He's coming down."

Floris picked up his print-out from the printer, turned around and looked back into the room. Everyone was standing up now. He just stood there for a minute composing himself for the arrival of the Director.

Sort of unexpectedly Floris said, "Sure thing, Sjoerd, you can have tomorrow off for the Keukenhof, and the day after, too, if you want. Won't be anything to do here."

Right after he said it, the Director rang to be let in, and all Hell broke loose.

After the Director had gone, I sent an informal to my contact back at the Fort.

Host has lost access to Cozy Bear.

Just before contact was lost, Cozy Bear was reading an article in "The Washington Post" about the Deputy Director NSA's comments at the Aspen Institute on 21 March, in which he disclosed US cooperation with host against Cozy Bear. Host and DSO agree that the loss of access was directly attributable to the information in the article. We watched it happen.

DSO just spent a very unpleasant half hour on the carpet with D/Host who made his very great displeasure with the disclosure known to DSO in no uncertain terms. This kind of thing was simply not done by reliable allies, said D/Host. D/Host asked if the US fully understands the vulnerability of this kind of access to disclosures in the press of the kind made by the Deputy Director. DSO replied that he could not answer for the Deputy Director, but that DSO was himself more than aware of the target's ability to read the Press and Mass Media, and how an open-source disclosure of this type could shatter the fragile technical access of a project like Cozy Bear.

D/Host reiterated the point that the neutralization of Cozy Bear's penetration of State, or of the DNC does not imply that our access to Cozy Bear was terminated. Collection had continued past those points, and was still active this morning before Cozy Bear read the article in *The Post*. The agreement with the Host calls for a 50-year DECLAS date, and access controls via a BIGOT List. The Deputy Director, therefore, had no business discussing the operation in an open forum like the Aspen Institute event while the project was on-going.

D/Host stated unequivocally that political expediency was not sufficient reason to compromise a project like Cozy Bear, especially since it was not the Deputy

Director's information to give away; it belonged to the Host, and the Host had not agreed to its disclosure. D/Host gave DSO to understand that all current collaboration with US would be reviewed in the very near future.

Expect an 'Eyes Only' to DIRNSA from D/Host on this topic before local CoB today. Expect him to DEMAND an unauthorized disclosure investigation.

We spent the next month rewriting the software package that had gotten us into Cozy Bear, removing all traces of things that would have been left by the version in the first penetration that could be identified. We set the language of all our editors to Russian. We made sure the post-dated compile times were during Moscow business hours, and not on a Russian holiday. We even included a 'white space' 'Easter Egg' in morse.

Our calling-card 'Easter Egg' said:

I code, therefore I am. Punch des Cartes.

Later, June 9th to be precise, the plot, as they say, got a little lumpy, like cold oatmeal.

"Igor," said Sasha on Bear Chat. "Did you catch the coverage of (named US person A)'s testimony to Congress in yesterday's *Washington Post*: 'White House lied about me, FBI'."

"Yes, I did," typed Igor. "I can't believe that there were people in the hearing room who gasped in surprise when (named US person A) said 'he had «no doubt» that the Russian government was behind the hack of the DNC. Don't these people read *The Post*? (named US person B) told everyone exactly how they knew it was us in April."

"And told us what to look for so we could kick them out," replied Sasha. "I still think we should send (named US person B) an Order of Lenin for services to the Russian Federation."

"Or a 'l337 Cozy 834Я' T-shirt," said Igor. "We could call it a 'retirement present' to be discreet."

"He doesn't look the T-shirt type," answered Sasha. "Definitely a suit."

"We should print up our own 'l337 Cozy 834Я' T-shirt," said Saskia, who had 'The Watch' and was following the conversation.

"Yellow letters on red, I think," said Menno.

"How about another line?" I asked. "l337 Cozy 834Я @127.0.0.1 on Ur C0m9u73r."

"What a hoot!" said Menno. "Who wants one?"

He had twenty orders in nothing flat, some of which were obviously 'trade goods' for people we owed favors to, well, at least five of mine were. Twenty was enough for a discount.[30]

---

[30] l337 Cozy 834Я T-shirts are available from:
https://www.cafepress.com/l337cozybeartshirt
(the first letter in 'l337' is a lower-case 'L').

Epilogue

After some serious horse trading, the Host reluctantly agreed to let me stay to the normal end of a three-year tour. They, however, flat-out refused to discuss the idea of a replacement with the Fort, and I wasn't about to pull in any personal markers to make it happen after word reached me that my re-assimilation assignment would be to the 'pre-publication review' shop at the Fort. Kathy and I decided to retire on a high note, and tell the Fort what it could do with an assignment to 'pre-publication review'. The view from retirement is great. I miss the work and the people who do it, but I don't miss the bureaucratic and political bullsh*t.

On the Monday after the Dutch success against Cozy Bear made headlines around the world, I got an eMail from Floris. It said:

> This weekend, right after the article on Thursday the 26th that blew our op against Cozy Bear was splattered all over the world press, there was a DDoS attack against all the big Dutch banks and the Dutch Tax Office. It originated from servers in Russia. Everybody is bending over backwards to say that the location of the servers is not indicative of the entity behind the attack and that it

has nothing to do with the press item on Cozy Bear. We haven't told anyone yet that the data stream used for the attack contained a 'white space' 'Easter Egg' in morse that said: "EB TVOIU AIVD 73 88 CB[31]."

"That sounds like Sasha all over," I smiled to myself.

Then I started to wonder how long it would take before news of the 'white space' 'Easter Egg' in the DDoS data stream hit the press.

Maybe the team just wouldn't tell anybody else about it. I hoped so. If they did, somebody would brief Congress, and it's leaky as a sieve. They just can't believe that the target reads the press they're leaking to, and would take steps to deny us the access that allows us to produce the intel that they are paying such big bucks for.

I still haven't seen anything in the media. Maybe Floris kept his mouth shut.

---

[31] Translator's note: Get F*cked, AIVD. 73 [Best Regards] 88 [Love & Kisses] C[ozy] B[ear].

Afterword

[U+200B][U+2003][U+2003][U+0020][U+200B][U+0020]
[U+0020][U+200B][U+200B][U+200B][U+200B][U+0020]
[U+200B][U+2003][U+0020][U+200B][U+200B][U+200B]
[U+2003][U+0020][U+200B][U+0020][U+0020][U+2003]
[U+2003][U+0020][U+200B][U+0020][U+2003][U+0020]
[U+0020][U+2003][U+0020][U+200B][U+200B][U+200B]
[U+200B][U+0020][U+200B][U+0020][U+0020][U+200B]
[U+0020][U+2003][U+200B][U+0020][U+200B][U+0020]
[U+2003][U+2003][U+0020][U+2003][U+200B][U+2003]
[U+2003][U+0020][U+0020][U+200B][U+2003][U+0020]
[U+2003][U+200B][U+0020][U+2003][U+200B][U+200B]
[U+0020][U+0020][U+200B][U+200B][U+200B][U+200B]
[U+0020][U+200B][U+0020][U+0020][U+200B][U+200B]
[U+0020][U+200B][U+200B][U+200B][U+0020][U+0020]
[U+200B][U+200B][U+2003][U+0020][U+200B][U+200B]
[U+200B][U+0020][U+0020][U+200B][U+2003][U+2003]
[U+200B][U+0020][U+2003][U+2003][U+2003][U+0020]
[U+2003][U+2003][U+200B][U+0020][U+2003][U+2003]
[U+2003][U+0020][U+0020][U+200B][U+2003][U+2003]
[U+200B][U+0020][U+2003][U+2003][U+2003][U+0020]
[U+200B][U+200B][U+200B][U+0020][U+200B][U+200B]
[U+200B][U+0020][U+200B][U+200B][U+2003][U+0020]
[U+2003][U+2003]

About the Author

F.W.A. van Nispen tot Pannerden (1983–) was born in Den Haag. He received a Master's Degree in Computer Science from the prestigious Eindhoven University of Technology in 2007. *In het hol van de Cozy Bear* is his debut novel. He lives in Zoetermeer with his wife Saskia and twins Menno and Mark.

A spokesperson for the AIVD declined to comment on the record as to whether Mr. van Nispen tot Pannerden is now, or ever has been, employed by the AIVD.

About the Translator

T.H.E. Hill served with the US Army Security Agency at Field Station Berlin in the mid-nineteen-seventies, after a tour at Herzo Base in the late nineteen-sixties. He is a three-time graduate of the Defense Language Institute (DLIWC) in Monterey, California, the alumni of which are called "Monterey Marys". The Army taught him to speak Russian, Polish, and Czech; three tours in Germany taught him to speak German, and his wife taught him to speak Dutch. He has been a writer his entire adult life, but now retired from Federal Service, he writes what he wants, instead of the things that others tasked him to write while he was still working.

Also by T.H.E. Hill:

- *Voices Under Berlin: The Tale of a Monterey Mary*
- *Berlin in Early Cold-War Army Booklets* (compiler)
- *The Day Before the Berlin Wall: Could We Have Stopped It? An Alternate History of Cold War Espionage*
- *Berlin in Early Berlin-Wall Era CIA, State Department, and Army Booklets* (compiler)
- *Reunification: A Monterey Mary Returns to Berlin*
- *Berlin in Détente-era Berlin Brigade Booklets* (compiler)

Made in the USA
Lexington, KY
05 January 2019